The Box

The Phaedra Chronicles

Charlotte Van

Publisher Charlotte Van

Book Cover by Cover by Art Saborio, AS Holdings and Assets Publishing, LLC

First Edition, 2024

CHAPTER 1

Before I tell you about the strange adventure I just walked out of, I should probably fill you in on what happened after the end of what I called The Spandex Murders.

It had taken a while for me to work out my issue with the fact that I'd killed a person, albeit one who'd been hellbent on killing me and perhaps also Tyler Powell, the object of her twisted passion. What brought me around was intense anger - anger at her for what she'd done to me. I was a mess until I'd finally swapped guilt and pain for my true, ornery self.

By the time all that settled down, Tyler and I had been lovers for just over a month. It seemed like I was staying at his place in Mill Valley more than at my own (and my brother Nick's) loft in San Francisco, and while it was great having such an amazing relationship, something felt off.

I hardly had any work at SIA, the private investigation company I worked for, as they didn't seem to quite know what to do with me after all the notoriety of solving the murder case for Tyler. So I was getting bored. Really bored.

And then there was the fact that Tyler and his band were going to be heading out on their farewell tour as Eros in a few days. He'd decided that doing the type of heavy metal Eros had become famous for was over and done. The tour had already been booked months before, so it had been re-branded as a last opportunity for fans to see Eros.

After the tour, he'd focus on his up-to-now private writing and stage a comeback, reinvented. Some of his team wanted to come along, but a few of them were already going to opt out.

The final tour was going to be a long one, and would take them to Europe, Asia, Australia, and South Africa, then the last leg across the U.S. He'd be gone for two months. I knew we were both wondering if our brand new relationship would withstand the separation, but then there's always Zoom, texts and emails, so it wasn't as if we would be totally separated.

We were still lying in bed, the morning sun filtering through the curtains. As we settled into holding each other, and my head rested on his chest, he sighed.

"You probably won't believe this, but that first night we had – it was the first time I'd ever literally slept with a woman I'd just had sex with."

"Really? Never?"

"Never. Up to now, my life has been a rock n' roll cliché. Sex with strangers. 'Wham, bam, thank you, ma'am.' 'One and done.' All the damned clichés.

"And afterwards, always climbing back into the hotel bed alone, thinking that was the way I wanted it. I'd convinced myself, because that's the way it always was."

He looked down at me and kissed my forehead sweetly.

"That's over with now."

He moved my hair away from my ear.

"Phaedra, I want you to move in here with me," he whispered. "Completely. Not just a few nights here and there."

I was stunned. I shifted to face him.

"What? You're asking me to give up the loft, my place?"

"You're barely there any more. I want you here."

"Ty, I'm not ready for that huge of a commitment, especially after just a month. We don't even really know each other well enough—"

"I think you're more ready than you'll admit, but you need to stop running away, using your freedom as an excuse. I mean, look at me, what I've been up until now. It's like my mother told me in her loving way, that I've 'flitted from flower to flower like a crazed butterfly'," in air quotes. "And she's right. But I've been making a fast transition away from that mindset, and I'm glad. What you've brought to my life is so much more satisfying, I can't help but want it and you every day."

I'd never been put in that situation before. Not even close. While I'd come to love the time and intimacy we'd been having together, frankly it was scaring me. And now he was asking me for a commitment I truly felt I couldn't make.

I looked him in the eyes.

"Ty, I don't think–"

"Okay, look. I know this is a huge thing for both of us, but especially for you. Don't decide right now. I'll be gone for two months. Take your time, and if you decide to go for it, you'll have plenty of time to move your stuff here and make me very happy when I get home."

I looked away and took a deep breath, exhaling louder than I intended.

"Ty, this is just way too much, way too soon."

"I disagree. It feels right when you're here with me. And when you're not here, it feels empty, like it used to before. I don't want that emptiness any more. You fill it."

"I enjoy our time together, Ty, but I—"

"It's about your job, isn't it? About being free and independent, with nothing tying you down."

"I thought that's how you felt, too. Nothing too serious to distract you from your own work. So don't criticize me for feeling the same way."

I got up from the bed and pulled on my bathrobe.

"I'm not criticizing you," he said defensively. "I'm just trying to figure out why you're resisting this so strongly. It makes sense for us to live together—"

I stared at him, not smiling.

"You're not even going to be here for two months! Why would I want to drag my stuff up here and sit around alone? At least at the loft there's Nick and the guys, and I'm close to work."

"What work? When was the last time you had an assignment?"

"That's beside the point—"

"Is it? How are you going to pay your part of the rent and bills, huh? Get a retail job?"

I glared at him.

"You have a very bizarre way of convincing a woman to move in with you, Tyler Powell. It's not working. Not one bit."

"I'm sorry. That was rude of me. What I want to say is that, if you're living here, you won't have those expenses."

"You just aren't getting it, are you? I am not interested in being a convenience – a live-in girlfriend who'll be here when you are, and invisible when you're not. Like Sarah was for Vic–"

"I can't believe you just said that!"

I thought about it and had to agree. It was cruel to have made the comparison, considering what we'd just been through with that whole mess.

"I'm sorry. You threw me for a huge loop, and I had a knee-jerk reaction. But I told you on that Sunday night that I wasn't interested in any commitment—"

"Things change. They did for me."

"Put yourself in my position, Ty. You're asked to move in with a famous musician notorious for his appetite for groupies. Wouldn't you tend to shy away because you didn't know if you could trust him when he's not with you?"

He got up and walked over to me, his brow furrowed.

"You really think I'd use you when I'm home, then go on the road and fuck any girl who comes near me?" I said nothing. "It's enlightening to find out that you think so little of me. And depressing."

"Depressing? What do you mean?"

"Do I really have to explain it to you?"

"You're going to be out on the road, Ty, and you've always—"

"I'm gonna stop you right there. You're thinking I'm going to still be in groupie mode. I get it. But like I've said, I'm done with that. All I want and need is *you* now. No other woman has ever given me what you've given me, and it's what I want. Two months of celibacy will be worth having you here to come home to."

I must have shown him an expression of disbelief, because he lifted my chin in order to make me look into his eyes.

"You're worried I'll succumb to temptation. You're going to have to trust me, Phaedra. That's all I can ask of you."

Despite his words, his eyes betrayed the hurt.

He drew on the jeans that were on the floor where he'd dropped them the night before, and headed downstairs. Not a great start to our day.

I got dressed – a ¾ length sundress and sandals, since the day was going to be warm – and I needed to feel as physically comfortable as possible, seeing whereas it might get even more emotionally uncomfortable in a few minutes.

I walked slowly down the stairs and took a deep breath as I rounded the corner to enter the kitchen. Ty was at the stove and I could smell bacon and espresso. I wondered at his bravery, cooking bacon while shirtless, but figured it was probably a result of his irritation with me. I watched as he turned to another pan and flipped a couple of pancakes.

"I'm lucky you're such a good cook," I said as I passed the stove and stood to his right. I hoped I could lighten the mood before any more serious conversation started.

"Great," he huffed, not looking up from the pan. "At least I'm doing *something* right, in your eyes."

"Ty—"

"Go ahead and sit down. Food's ready."

The chill coming off of him was palpable, and I hated it. We wouldn't get very far if we both shored up our proverbial walls.

I sat at the table and watched as he put my plate and cup down with all the feeling of an impersonal restaurant server. He went back to the stove and returned with his own food, sitting across from me without a word. The sunlight through the diamond pane windows illuminated him from behind, giving him a bright aura, despite his mood.

How was I going to deal with this? Chances were, neither of us would want to give ground, so I figured I needed to make a strategic move.

"I'm sorry," I said quietly, looking directly at him. He raised his eyes to meet mine, just as I'd hoped. "I didn't mean for my reaction to hurt you. You caught me by surprise, that's all."

"I didn't expect it to come as such a shock to you, Phaedra." He looked down into his cup as he took a sip of his espresso. "I get the impression that I'm deeper into this relationship than you are."

I reached over and put my hand over his.

"I want to be with you, Ty, but we've only been together a month! Moving in with you like you're asking me to—it's too quick for me. You already know me well enough to know how I am."

I stood up and moved my chair over next to him and sat back down as he took a bite of pancake and followed it with a sip of espresso, not looking at me. I reached over and put my fingertips on his chin, raising it to make him look at me.

"Understand this. I'm not saying no."

"What does that mean?"

"It means that we can compromise. There's no reason for me to move in here full time without you here. That will give me time to think long and hard about what you're asking for, and I promise to have an answer for you when you get back from the tour."

Ty looked to his left, out to the pool and patio, then back at me.

"I have an idea, but I want you to let me finish telling you what it is before you raise any objections."

"You're assuming I'll object?"

"I'm assuming you'll have an opinion."

"That's an easy assumption, Mr. Powell. I'm chock full of opinions."

He actually smiled.

"That you are. I admire you for that, you know. I admire your tenacity."

I reached out and stroked his stubbly cheek.

"Thank you. That's the first time anyone, especially a man, has actually appreciated what my father called 'my spunk'."

We both laughed. The tension that had been so palpable was slowly dissipating, and we smiled silently at each other.

"Okay, here's my idea. Stay at the loft as much as you want while I'm gone, but I'd like you to come up here at least 2 days a week to make sure everything's okay, and to check on the housekeepers and the gardener. Stay overnight if you want, use the pool, everything. But what I want to do is pay you for what we'll call 'housesitting'."

"Pay me? That's—"

"Uh-uh. I told you to let me finish, so hush." He got up to make another espresso and motioned to ask if I wanted one as well, to which I nodded.

"We talked briefly about how you're not getting work from SIA, and certainly not enough to keep your bills paid. I don't want you to have to go out and try to find a job that will be a waste of your time, when you're capable of so much. Paying you to keep an eye on the house will keep you going and give you the space to look for a job you can sink your pearly whites into. I just want to help you, Phaedra, if you'll let me."

"That's actually not a bad idea, Ty. And it would give me the freedom to pick up any tidbit jobs SIA might toss my way while you're gone. I appreciate your concern. I really do."

He placed our fresh espressos on the table and sat back down, facing me. An impish smile lit up his face.

"Great. But I have a condition that goes along with this idea."

I rolled my eyes and took a sip of my coffee.

"You and your fucking conditions!" I laughed.

"Hey, you've had a couple yourself, lady! But I think you'll like this one. I know I will."

"And what's that?"

"That regardless of whatever schedule you set up for coming up here, you'll be here when I get back from this damned tour, and that you'll be waiting for me in our bed, naked. How's that for a condition?"

"An unnecessary one," I answered in what I considered to be a seductive tone. I leaned over and kissed his cheek. "I planned to do that all on my own, without prompting."

"Good," he growled, reaching over and pulling my face to his for a deep, prolonged kiss. "That gives me something enticing to look forward to, although I'll need to Zoom or Skype you frequently to have you remind me about it."

"I'm glad we got that worked out for now. I've got to get on the phone to the caterer to make sure everything's good to go for the staff party later."

He took my hand to his lips.

"How soon are the catering people due?"

"In about an hour. Why?"

"Why do you think?" He stood and pulled me up into his arms. "Shall we try the couch?"

CHAPTER 2

It was our last morning. He'd be off to the airport in a matter of hours.

We'd slept the whole night with me in his arms, my head on his chest. I could feel him begin to stir as the morning light hit the closed curtain.

He moved out from under me and sat on the edge of the bed, looking back at me.

"Sorry, sweetheart. I need to pee. I'll be right back."

I gaped as he walked to the bathroom. That was the first time he'd called me sweetheart. It was such an unexpected and intimate expression, I was shocked.

When he returned, he knelt next to me on the bed and bent down to kiss me, one hand cradling my cheek. Then he laid down with his back to me, and I was soon spooning him. My right arm reached across his shoulder and chest, and he drew that hand to his lips.

"These are our last hours together before I have to leave. We need to make the most of them." He moved my hand down to grasp his arousal. "We need some more to tide us over."

A while later, as Ty's head was resting on my arm, nuzzled against my breast, I had another of my now infamous epiphanies.

I realized with a depth previously unknown to me that I was going to miss this intimacy of our lovemaking. I wasn't used to allowing this kind of needy vulnerability in myself, and I was pretty sure it was the same for Ty.

"I don't know about you, but I'm hungry," he finally said as he turned, propped up on his elbow, staring at me. "However, I do believe we've completely missed breakfast."

"That we did," I responded, chuckling lightly and stroking the heavy stubble on his face. "How about I make us lunch after we shower?"

"I'd like that. Maybe while I'm gone, you can work on upping your culinary skills."

"*Excuse me*?" I exclaimed, swatting his bare forearm. "My culinary skills are just fine, thank you very much!"

"But not as good as mine. I dare you to best me."

"Oh, you're on, mister! You just wait."

"I wish I didn't have to. I hate having to leave."

"We can video chat and Facetime whenever possible. That will help."

"But it's not touching you, making love with you."

"No, it isn't, but let's not dwell on that. You have to leave in a couple of hours, so let's just enjoy each other's company over lunch."

Not too much later we were in the kitchen and Ty had just finished making us both espresso. He placed the cups on the table and sat. I stood at the oak island, assembling our sandwiches from the whole grain bread we'd picked up at our favorite bakery in town, smearing garlicky mayonnaise on one slice, Dijon mustard on the other, then layering on slices of Havarti, thin-sliced smoked turkey breast, crispy bacon, and lettuce and tomato fresh from the garden.

I plated them and brought them over to the table. Ty took a big bite out of his and rolled his eyes dramatically.

"I have to admit that you do make one hell of a sandwich, Ms. McCaffrey."

"Why thank you, Mr. Powell. Does that excuse me then from your culinary improvement challenge?"

"Let's just say it's optional. Surprise me when I get back home."

When we'd finished, I stood to take the dishes to the sink, but turned and looked him in the eye.

"I want to apologize again for my knee-jerk reaction when you first asked me to move in." He reached out and touched my arm. "You threw me off-guard and I overreacted. I'm sorry. I just...I just don't do well with surprises."

"I can tell. Surprises keep you from being able to be in control of what's going on around you. I could tell that the first day we worked together. I knew you were going to be a hell of a challenge."

"Oh, you did, did you? Is that why you kept pushing my buttons?"

"I kept pushing them because I was looking for the one that would bring you to where we are now."

"So that was your plan, was it?"

"Yep. But regardless of what you just said about not liking surprises, I'm afraid I'll be tossing them at you relentlessly from now on."

I sighed dramatically.

"Oh well, if you must," I said, smiling.

Inwardly at that moment, I was thinking about how I'd never really had surprises growing up. My mother cared only about herself and how to maneuver herself deeper in the infamous San Francisco social elite. My father, while generally wonderful to me, was too absorbed in his high level legal battles to attend to anything as trivial as surprises for his two children. Birthdays were minimally celebrated, and the only small surprises then were from Grandma McCaffrey and Great Aunt Mary, her sister.

It sounded like I was going to have to adjust my surprises attitude.

I stood at the sink, cleaning the few dishes we'd dirtied, when I felt Ty come up behind me. He put one arm around my waist, reaching around to my front with the other.

"I have a little present for you."

His hand held a black velvet-covered box about the size of a paperback book. He opened it.

It was a necklace – a delicate rose-gold chain, the ends of which held the word 'fierce' in rose-gold script lettering, set with pale peach stones.

"I had this custom-made for you, to show you my appreciation of the woman you are. I chose rose gold because I knew it would look beautiful with your hair. The gemstones are Morganite, to match. Let me."

I'm sure my mouth must have been hanging open. It was beautiful. But how did he know that Morganite, with its pale peach color, was one of my favorite stones? Even Nick didn't know that.

Ty set the box down on the counter, removed the necklace, and came around behind me, fastening the clasp as he put the necklace around my neck. He turned me around and smiled as he admired his present.

"Perfect," he whispered, kissing my neck. "And it goes beautifully with your skin tone, too."

I reached up with both my hands and pulled his face into a deep kiss.

"Thank you! I love it!"

"It's how I think of you – fierce and passionate. I need to take a few pictures so I can look at them while I'm away from you."

He pulled his cell phone from his pants pocket and took a few shots, capturing my smiling face in some of them.

I had to admit that it was one of the nicest gifts I'd ever been given.

"Damn! Look what time it is! Oscar will be here in about half an hour!"

Oscar, his preferred and longtime driver, would be driving him to the airport to catch his flight to Tokyo.

Ty headed down to the studio to grab his favorite black Fender Stratocaster, which he always traveled with as carry-on. I zipped upstairs to double-check that he had everything he'd need for two months in his luggage. His trusty backpack sat on the bed, waiting for his laptop and accessories to be added to it. He came up the stairs, two at a time.

"I'll take the two suitcases down if you'll pack up the laptop and chargers, and my iPhone accessories in the backpack. I've got the phone."

"Will do."

The guitar case and two suitcases were by the front door, and I set his backpack next to them, ready to go. We stood there, staring mutely at each other, not knowing what to say in the moment, when the doorbell rang, making me jump.

It was Oscar of course – the older black gentleman (and I call him that very purposefully, because that's what I've come to know him to be) Ty had been using for a few years as his preferred driver. Because of Ty's frequent use of his services, Oscar had been able to buy his own Lincoln Town Car.

"Time to head out, Mr. Powell," he said as Ty opened the door. He picked up both suitcases. "I'll put these in the trunk. I know you like to keep the rest with you inside the car."   "Thank you, Oscar," Ty said, then turning to me. "Well, this is it. Goodbye for now." He pulled me into his arms and buried his face in my hair. "I hate this so much."

He backed up just enough to let us kiss goodbye, which took a couple of minutes.

I moved so that my mouth nuzzled his left ear. I felt him shiver at the touch.

"Be safe," I whispered, and without thinking, added "sweetheart."

He stepped back, looking astonished, as if he didn't believe what he'd heard me say. I hardly believed it myself, but I saw a slight smile on his face but sadness in his eyes.

He picked up the guitar case and backpack, and walked out the door. I stood in the doorway and watched as he put his gear into the back seat and got in the front passenger seat. He lowered the window and looked over at me. I blew him an obligatory kiss, and closed my eyes so that I couldn't see his reaction.

Two months...

CHAPTER 3

My iPhone was ringing.

Still mostly asleep, I reached out to the nightstand and picked it up, opening my sleepy eyes to see what time it was.

2:14 a.m.

"Who the fuck?" I grumbled, annoyed. But then I looked at who was calling at that ungodly hour.

It was Ty, of course, wanting to FaceTime.

I smiled in spite of my initial annoyance and slid the 'Accept' button. His face appeared on the screen, smiling broadly.

"Hey, are you there? It's so dark on your end, I can't see you," he said, looking concerned. I could see he was dressed for a show.

"That's because it's 2:15 in the morning, asshole, and you just awakened me out of a very nice dream!"

He closed his eyes and groaned.

"Oh man! I'm sorry, Phae! I'm so wrapped up in this first show of the tour, I spaced on the time difference between Tokyo and California. I promise not to make that mistake again, wherever we are."

"It's okay. I just get grumpy when I'm awakened in the middle of a dream." I brought my phone closer to my face, hoping the light from his end would make me visible to him, but it didn't. "I'd much rather talk with you. I can always catch more sleep when we're done."

"Good." I could see him squinting, as if he were trying hard to see something. "So where are you? I can't tell."

"What do you mean where am I?" I knew, of course, but he didn't need to know that.

"I'm just curious which bed you're in."

"What does it matter?"

"Oh, come on! Humor me."

I laughed and gave him a provocative look, one eyebrow raised.

"Okay, here's a hint," I said, turning my phone to capture the comforter that covered me. Hopefully there'd be enough light that he'd see the Star Wars print on his favorite bedcover.

A broad smile lit his face as I turned the phone back to me.

"It makes me both happy and sad to see you in my bed."

"Why sad?"

"Simple. Because I'm not there with you. I see you're wearing the necklace I gave you."

"I haven't taken it off since you put it around my neck. I even took the chance that it wouldn't turn green when I showered."

"Cheeky bitch!" he laughed. "You know damned well it's real!"

"Of course I do," I responded, taking on a serious look. I wasn't sure he could see it, but I really didn't want to turn on the light next to me. "Wearing it keeps me close to you, just like I'm sure you intended."

"That's right." He looked to his left at someone. "When I get home, I'll be in the studio a lot and rehearsing, but we'll spend time—"

"Ty, don't worry about all that now. Don't distract yourself, especially so early in the tour. You need to focus."

"I like that you get me, that you understand what I'm doing and what I *will* be doing. Your support means so much to me."

"Likewise, Ty. I think you understand how important it is to me to be independent and self-sufficient, and I appreciate it."

"Yes, I do understand and I respect that. But that will never stop me from wanting to do things for you, so you're just going to have to get used to it."

"That's a two-way street, Mr. Powell. So if there's anything I can do to help you on this end, just let me know."

I could tell that he'd put his hand over his phone's mic and was talking with someone there at the Tokyo venue.

"I will. I've gotta go. The stage manager's giving me the stink eye because it's time for sound check and they're all waiting for me. I'll call you tomorrow, at an appropriate time for you, to let you know how it went. Sweet dreams, love."

I turned off my phone and turned on my side, wishing he were there to spoon or be spooned by.

I continued to wonder how I'd come to be so enrobed in this brand new relationship so quickly. Actually, how at all.

Where had my relationship/commitment phobia disappeared to?

It was now 5 days after Ty's departure, and I was floating in the pool.

I'd just gotten back from the city, picking up a few more basics from the loft. I was going to leave the rest of my stuff there, since I already had most of what I'd need whenever I'd stay at Ty's.

Nick had questioned me as to why I wasn't taking all of it up to Ty's. Was I expecting we wouldn't last? He even accused me of self-sabotage and fear of real commitment. I'd ignored him.

Ty and I had cleared some space in his huge walk-in closet, so now I had a selection of my clothes hanging and stored in drawers opposite his things. I stood there looking at it all, still in a bit of shock that I'd moved some of my things in with a man so quickly. It seemed so unlike me, and yet...

For as much as I'd gotten done in the day, it was still only 1 in the afternoon, and I was floating aimlessly in the pool, my mind phasing in and out of blankness.

What was happening to me? What was I doing? Nothing.

I'd gone through a "nothing phase" when we'd hidden out in Tahoe just a couple of weeks before, and it had taught me that doing nothing of any consequence was very, very unhealthy for me. I found that I don't do at all well having time to ruminate on my life and its direction. Idle time gives me a fucking headache.

There on the water in the early afternoon sun, I decided to call my boss Anne at SIA to basically beg her for work – any kind of work. Without work, I'd go stir crazy over 2 months of no Tyler around to distract me.

There was nothing to do around the house other than cleaning, and Ty had 2 ladies who came in weekly to do that. So I didn't even feel like a house-sitter. More like a houseguest minus the host.

What had my life come to? Certainly nothing like I'd ever envisioned or planned.

It was imperative that I reclaim myself, for sanity's sake.

I paddled the float over to the ladder and climbed out of the pool, wrapping myself in the large red towel that I'd left on the concrete. I sat down at the oak table next to the barbeque, and picked up my cell phone.

I hit Anne's private office number and waited for her to answer. What I got was a message saying that she was out of town for the rest of the week, and that any important issues be communicated to her co-director, David Blake.

So I dialed David's number.

"Phaedra! Good to hear from you!" his deep voice said. "What can I do for you?"

"I tried calling Anne but her message said she's out of town."

"Right. She and Jen had to fly to St. Louis for a family funeral."

"Sorry to hear that." I took a deep breath. "I need to ask a favor."

"A favor? I'll see what I can do. What is it you need?"

"Work. Anything."

"What's going on? Is everything okay?"

"You may have heard that I may be moving in with Tyler, but he left a few days ago on a two-month world tour, so I'm alone when I'm at his place. And I'm already going stir crazy, David. I need to work."

"I understand, but we're barely keeping the operatives busy."

"I don't expect regular operative's work. I could do research, grave-yard shifts on surveillances no one else wants to do, hell, I'd even play receptionist and answer the phones. You could force Alice to finally take a vacation."

David laughed at that. Alice never seemed to take one.

"I get it. Let me talk with Claudia. Since she's the office manager, she'll have a handle on what all needs to get done around here. How about you come in around noon tomorrow and the three of us will talk about it over lunch."

"Come through for me, Claudia," I'd said out loud as the call ended. "Please."

CHAPTER 4

Two days later, I sat in David Blake's office, waiting for him to arrive. I twiddled my thumbs, wondering what assignment he had for me. He and Claudia had been kind enough to throw me some bones to keep me somewhat busy while Ty was out on tour.

A few minutes later, he arrived, along with a young man who looked to be in his mid-twenties. David sat behind his desk and motioned for the young man to sit in the chair to my left.

"Phaedra, this is my nephew, Logan Blake. He's coming on board provisionally."

"Provisionally?" I asked. Since that wasn't normal procedure, I immediately speculated a little nepotism was involved in the arrangement.

"We're going to see if investigation is something he can function within the confines of."

"I don't follow."

"Uncle David means he isn't sure I can take it seriously," the young guy offered, turning and staring at me. "He's quite familiar with my track record when it comes to careers."

I looked over at David, my eyebrows raised.

"For god's sake, Logan, let's not get off on the wrong foot." He glared at his nephew, and then turned his eyes to me. "Phaedra, I want you to show Logan the ropes on surveillance. Are you available to go out tonight? I know it's short notice."

"Sure. I just need to text Ty that I won't be able to Facetime tonight. I'll call him tomorrow. They're in Singapore today – or tomorrow over there, I guess. Then they'll head to Sydney in a couple of days."

"So who are we talking about?" Logan interjected, a cocky smile on his face.

I already didn't like him. I could tell that this was going to be a bitch.

"Phaedra's significant other, if that term's still being used these days. Enough of that. Let's go over the case, then you two can go to the break room to get into details."

Ten minutes later, we were entering the small break room. I sat at the table, setting down my new leather shoulder bag (a gift from Ty to replace my natty old college one). Logan maneuvered to sit next to me, but I motioned him to sit across from me. He complied with what looked to me like a sarcastic smile.

"So this boyfriend of yours is in Singapore, eh?"

I looked him directly in the eye, purposefully furrowing my brow.

"Let's get this straight right now. My personal life is none of your damned business, nor is yours any of mine.

"My job is to train you in surveillance, nothing more. You either focus and behave professionally, or we're done. Got it?"

"Okay, okay!" He leaned forward and set his chin on his raised hands. "So what's the deal with spying on people?"

I sighed deeply, rolled my eyes, and shook my head.

'Why me, David?' I moaned to myself. 'What did I ever do to deserve this?'

That first night of surveillance was typically dull and without any incident, which made it all the more tortuous. Logan did nothing but bitch about how fucking boring it was, and groused about having to make hourly notes, even though nothing had happened. I explained that it was procedure and to just deal with it.

Unfortunately, we were sent out two more times that week, and both, of course, were equally annoying. I was determined to tell David that I had important personal business to attend to for the next several days, even though that would be a lie posing as an excuse to remove Tonight, down at China Basin, just 10 to 1. A short one."

I seriously didn't want to, but David and Anne had been generous to give me enough Logan from my presence.

"Just one more, Phaedra? Please," David pleaded when I told him. "Then you're done. work to keep me from going stir crazy. And I needed the small income to supplement my "house sitting" salary from Ty to keep my bills paid.

So I picked Logan up in front of the building at 9:45 and drove down to the surveillance location in the mostly deserted China Basin. After about an hour of sitting and observing, and snacking on what we'd each brought for ourselves, Logan shifted in the passenger seat to face me.

"So where's the boyfriend now? Bora Bora?"

I stared at him.

"If your memory's so bad that you can't remember what I told you about minding your own business, then this is definitely not the career for you."

"Just wouldn't want him showing up in the middle of this."

"Middle of what?" I demanded.

"This," he whispered, grabbing my chin, turning my face toward him, and kissing me aggressively.

I grabbed his wrist, twisted it, and threw it down into his lap.

"*Get out*," I growled, looking him in the eye as he rubbed his wrist.

"You're kidding. You wouldn't."

"I said *get out*!"

"You can't just leave me here! How will I get back to the office to get my car?"

"That's not my problem, asshole. What did you expect, blind acceptance of your juvenile advances? Give me a break."

"You're just not into it because I'm not your millionaire rocker boyfriend. Yes, I've looked you two up online. I'm sure you want to hold on tight to that fat meal ticket."

That broke the dragon's back (a camel wasn't enough to match my anger). I pulled the keys from the ignition, got out of the car, walked over to the passenger side, and opened the door.

"Grab your bag and get the hell out of my car. *Now*."

He got out begrudgingly, stunned. As he stepped away from the car, I slammed the door shut and went back over to the driver's seat. As I closed the door and locked it, I started the ignition. I leaned over and opened the window next to him.

"Feel free to finish out the remaining two hours. If you're lucky, an Uber or Lyft driver might be willing to come out here. Or not."

"Uncle David's going to be royally pissed at you for this!"

"No, he won't," I responded, smiling. "David knows me."

And I drove off, leaving him there. I headed to the loft, to sleep in my own bed. When I'd settled in under the covers, I texted David, letting him know in no uncertain terms that I was never going to work with Logan again, that SIA should get rid of him as a potential liability, and I was very clear as to why.

CHAPTER 5

A week later, I was working at my desk in the SIA office doing research when my cell phone rang next to me. As I picked it up, I saw it was a call from Rob Helsing, Ty's bass player.

My first reaction was one of alarm. Why would Rob be calling me? Had something happened on the tour? Was Ty okay?

My finger shook a little as I hit Accept. It was a video call, and I hoped I looked decent. I got up from the desk and walked out to the hall for privacy.

"Hey, Phaedra!" Rob said cheerily. That relieved my worry right away. It looked like he was probably calling from his hotel room in Perth, where the itinerary said they'd be that day. "I hope you don't mind me calling you like this. I mean, we don't really know each other that well yet. Anyway, I was just talking to my wife a few minutes ago, checking in with her and the kids like I do every day, and she told me I should call you."

"Call me about what, Rob?" I asked. Why would his wife want him to call me? "What's going on? Is everything okay?"

"Oh, yeah, everything's fine. In fact, better than it ever was before."

"Then what?"

"My wife Shelly reminded me what it was like for her when I first went out on tour several years ago. She worried that I'd be tempted to, well, screw around on her. Y'know, it's the reputation touring musicians have had for decades really, but it's more often than not an undeserved one. I assured her every time she sounded doubtful that I would never do that to her, or now to our two kids. My family means everything to me."

"So she told you to call me about Ty?"

"Yeah. To let you know, since I'm with him almost all day, every day, and I know him really well, that he's a totally changed guy. Before, he'd go right from a show to scouting out which chick he'd take back to the hotel. On this tour, after the show we either all go out for a late dinner, or Ty goes right to his hotel room to tweak songs or write new ones. And to call you."

"I'm glad I've had a positive influence on him."

"It's more than that, Phaedra. Here's an example. Last night, as we were leaving the venue, this cute blonde came up to Tyler and started getting really aggressive about wanting you-know-what. He told her no right away, but she wasn't letting up. Steve was about to have security get rid of her when Tyler looked her straight in the eye and told her he would never cheat on his true love. That shut her up and she left. We all smiled, and I high-fived him."

I was tearing up, which I'd never ever done anywhere near so much before being with Tyler Powell. I wiped the tears away with my free hand.

"Tell Shelly I really appreciate what she did. She and I will have to get together soon and commiserate."

"I'll let her know. I'm sure she'd like that, since none of the other guys are in relationships. Maybe we can all get together after the tour, and you can meet the kids, too."

"Sounds like a plan," I said, smiling now that the tears were gone. "Thanks, Rob. See you soon. Take care."

"You, too."

A few days later, I was in Anne's office, talking with her about continuing to do work for SIA periodically. I would be stopping at Parducci's Ristorante afterward, to have a quick bite and pick up a full dinner-to-go to take home, as I'd be picking Ty up at SFO in a couple of hours.

Finally!

We'd been apart for about a month, thanks to that damned world tour, but since some of the Australian shows had been canceled due to a fraudulent promoter, he was able to come home for about a week before he'd have to fly to Johannesburg to pick up the tour again.

I wasn't going to let him go anywhere for at least a couple of days.

Anne's phone rang, a call from Alice the receptionist in the lobby.

"Phaedra," Anne said, her eyebrows arched. "Alice says Tyler is in the lobby right now with his luggage."

"What? He must have caught an earlier flight and wanted to surprise me. That man! I hope you don't mind if we cut our meeting short."

Anne laughed.

"Are you kidding? You two haven't been with each other in weeks. Let's get down there and say hi."

As we headed down the stairs, I heard Ty's voice, raised and angry. What was going on?

"Whoever the hell you are, I don't appreciate what you're implying about Phaedra! Not that it's any of your business, but we have a committed relationship—"

"Yeah, right!" The voice belonged to Logan. Oh hell. "With your reputation, you think she's gonna believe you didn't help yourself in the weeks you left her alone? Ever think maybe she'd be helping herself, too?"

We were now where we could see the two men standing by Alice's reception desk, less than a foot from each other. I could feel Ty's rage from where I stood. Neither of them had seen us.

"Think about it, dude. I've been training with her, for hours alone with a beautiful woman in a car doing surveillance. Things happen—"

Ty grabbed him by the collar of his shirt. I would have done it myself, had I been close enough to the jerk.

"Don't you *dare* talk about her like that!" Ty growled in Logan's face.

"Logan! My office! Now!" Anne called out, furious.

I headed down the rest of the stairs as Ty let Logan go and he started toward his boss. As we passed each other, I glared at him and did something I now feel was a bit childish. I gave him the finger in a forceful upward gesture.

Ty and I moved quickly to each other, and he took my face in his hands, kissing me long and deeply. We wrapped our arms around each other.

"What are you doing here so early? I was going to pick you up in a couple of hours."

"I couldn't wait. I caught an earlier flight." He kissed me again. "After weeks of celibacy, I wanted to get home to you ASAP. Speaking of which, let's go home. *Now*."

I chuckled as I kissed him on the cheek.

"Not quite yet. I pre-ordered dinner to take home from Parducci's nearby. I'll just need to run in and grab it, since I've already paid. Then we can head home."

Ty lifted my chin and looked me in the eyes, his sparkling with a smile.

"If you think we're going to eat when we get home, you are very sadly mistaken, my dear. Ain't no way!"

CHAPTER 6

Two days later, I was coming in from the vegetable garden out back with makings for a salad, and was struck by what I could only describe as a tense vibe in the air.

Since he'd been back, Ty hadn't said anything about wanting me to move in, but I'd been sensing it hovering in his mind. I was hoping it wouldn't emerge before he had to leave again in a few days, that we could maintain the warmth of being together for this little while without bringing up a sore subject (for me).

So, of course, when he came into the kitchen a few minutes later, I could see the tension in his face and eyes, and I knew he was going to broach the subject.

"I'm wondering if you've made your decision yet. You said you'd—"

"What I said, Ty, was that I'd have an answer for you when you got done with the tour. That's not now."

"Why the hell not?" he demanded, moving in front of me, his arms crossed. "What's so difficult about this? I don't get it!"

I found myself becoming impatient and irritated with how pushy he was being. He was stomping on my independent/self-sufficient button, causing me to react stronger than I would have otherwise, but he was pushing it.

"Am I just a convenience for you?" I asked with an edge, my back turned from him.

"What's that supposed to mean?"

"We talked about this before you left, and I said something about how I'd feel like a convenient substitute if I move in."

He glared at me so hard, I could feel it even though my back was to him.

"I can't believe that's what you think about me. I...after everything we've been through together, you actually feel that way?"

"It's how it's feeling to me right now."

"No, you're just afraid of what's really happening with us, and you don't believe that I'm actually serious."

"I'm not afraid."

He walked quickly in front of me and grabbed my shoulders so I couldn't turn away again.

"Yes, you are. Maybe you should retreat to your little brick bunker in the city and hide out. That way you can avoid any kind of real relationship, let alone one with *me*."

I closed my eyes and took a deep breath. I opened them again, looking him straight in the eyes.

"Does that mean you want me to leave?"

"No, I don't *want* you to, but under the current circumstances, I think you seriously *need* to."

"Well then, I guess I'll pack up what little I've brought up here and get out of your hair."

I turned and started up the stairs to the bedroom. I glanced back at him, but his back was to me, his arms crossed against his chest in a gesture of resolute resignation.

"It should only take me about 15 minutes. Do you want your keys back?"

"No. We still have a deal. You'll still come here a couple of times a week until I get back. The gardener will need guidance in planting the vegetable garden for Fall, and the cleaning ladies—" He turned and looked up at me, his face blank. "I'll have Maggie get you a check every week."

How quickly we'd degenerated from lovers to employer and house-sitter.

What was wrong with us that our new relationship was so fragile, so brittle that it could break into pieces so easily?

As I packed my suitcase, I wondered if he was thinking the same.

When I came downstairs and put my suitcase and purse next to the door, he got up from the kitchen table and walked toward me. What was he going to say?

"Just so you know, I've changed my flight to Johannesburg. I'm flying out at 11 tomorrow morning. There's no point in me sticking around here now."

I took a couple of steps toward him and stopped about a foot away. I didn't know what to say or do, but I had to do something.

"Be safe," I whispered, reaching out and stroking the stubble on his cheek, then drew back.

I didn't look up to see his response, but turned, picked up my suitcase and purse, opened the door and left.

There were no phone calls, no texts, no FaceTimes. Nothing.

He'd been gone for over 3 weeks with no word.

We seemed to be a classic example of two very stubborn personalities, neither of whom wanted to be the first to make a move toward reconciliation. It was an unhealthy impasse, and I was sure we both knew it.

Even thinking about it for very long was exhausting and depressing.

But at the same time, I was begrudgingly admitting to myself that I missed him. That I missed *us*.

We'd made a mistake. No, *I'd* made a mistake, and I needed to own it.

Every day that passed and I slept alone in my bed in the old warehouse apartment, I came to the growing realization that what I really wanted was to be sleeping with my lover ...anywhere.

I needed to fix it, and I'd make the first move, damn it. I was done playing this foolish damn game.

It was 8:30 pm when my phone rang. I picked it up and looked at the screen.

It read 'Ty'. I slid 'Accept'.

"Well, hello there," I said, purposefully nonchalantly.

"I wasn't sure you'd answer."

"Of course I would."

"Really?"

"Yes, really, Ty. I've been waiting."

"Waiting? For me to call?

"For anything."

I heard him sigh.

"Oscar picked me up at SFO. We're on the bridge now, so I'll be home soon. Will you come up so we can talk? Please?"

"I'll see you there," I said, and disconnected.

Little did he know that I was already there and waiting per his request weeks earlier.

CHAPTER 7

I heard the front door open, and Ty's and Oscar's voices as Ty turned off the security system and turned on the lights.

"That should be all your luggage, Mr. Powell," I heard Oscar say, then the door closed.

I peeked through the crack in the bedroom door, and saw Ty pull his laptop out of his backpack, heard him sigh, then saw he was starting up the stairs.

I rushed back to the bed, bent my knees to my naked chest, and pulled the covers up just enough to show my naked shoulders.

I was setting my scene. It was my plan, my surprise for him, since he didn't know I was already there. I was going to enjoy his reaction, since I knew pretty well what it would be.

I watched, smiling, as the door opened, but saw that he wasn't looking at the bed. He was staring at the fire in the fireplace, which I'd lit a half hour before, knowing it would throw him off.

"What the fuck! Why's the firepl—"

Mid-word, his eyes moved from the fireplace to the bed, and he saw me.

"Welcome home," I said in my best seductive purr.

"You're here," he said quietly, his eyes widening. "When I called, I wasn't sure you'd actually come."

"If you'll remember, when you left the first time, you made me promise to be here in your bed, naked, when you got home. So here I am."

I lowered the covers, exposing myself. He set the laptop down on a nearby chair, tore off his beloved leather jacket and threw it on the floor, rushing over to the bed. He sat down on the edge next to me, and reached out for my left hand.

"I'm sorry," he whispered.

We touched fingers, clasping them together.

"I'm sorry, too."

My breasts freed from the covers, I stretched out and brought my lips to his. He gasped.

"Oh damn!" he exclaimed, pulling his black t-shirt over his head and tossing it in the general direction of his jacket. "I was afraid that after what happened when you walked out the door—"

I cut him off with two fingers on his lips.

"We can talk about all that in the morning, at breakfast. I have other plans for you right now, Mr. Powell."

I moved my hand from his lips down to the waistband of his jeans, unbuttoning them. I started pulling on the zipper, but stopped, a move meant to signal him to stand and divest himself of the rest of his clothes.

He got the hint immediately.

Moments later, he threw the covers back completely, and pushed my bent legs apart, kneeling between them. He leaned in to kiss me forcefully.

"God, I missed you!" he said as his lips left mine and moved to my left breast.

"Then show me just how much," I whispered, running my fingers through his long hair.

"With pleasure. Great pleasure."

The next hour or so proved to me that I'd made the right decision.

We lay there facing each other, our faces softened with satisfaction.

"That reminded me of our first time," he said softly, running the back of his hand over my cheek.

"I think you mean our second first time."

His eyebrows raised and furrowed at that.

"Yeah, I'd rather forget that first first. I was a jerk."

"That you were, but you were on auto-pilot. You weren't seeing *me*, you were just seeing another faceless body to use."

"Let's not go there again, and don't try to make excuses for what I did. I'd like to think we've gotten past that."

"We have. Now, I suspect you need to get your beauty sleep, sir. The tour's over, you're home, and you need to rest." I reached over and tousled his hair playfully. "So who is going to spoon whom?"

Laughing, he grabbed me and flipped me onto my other side, scooting over to mold his body to mine.

"You have no idea how much I've been wanting to do this and fall asleep in my own bed with my arm resting on you. Bliss. I need to write a song about this."

We both chuckled at that.

It didn't take long for him to start snoring softly. I sighed, closed my eyes, and made my decision.

When I went down to the kitchen the next morning after my shower, casually resplendent in my purple yoga pants and lavender tee, I could smell that Ty was already at work making breakfast. I went over to him at the stove and gave him a kiss on the cheek.

Apparently that wasn't good enough for him, and he grabbed me around the waist with his left arm while his right hand held tongs. A solid kiss on the lips was what he required, and I was happy to oblige.

"You didn't have to make breakfast," I said as I reached to grab his espresso to take a sip. "It's your first morning back. I would have happily done it so that you can just take it easy."

He smiled and took back his cup.

"I wanted to. I've missed cooking in my kitchen, especially after 2 months of hotel, restaurant and venue catering food. That gets old real fast."

"I can imagine," I said, moving from his arms to the espresso machine to make my own drink. "So what are you making besides bacon?"

"I was in the mood for waffles. That okay with you?"

I must have made a face, because he laughed.

"Tell me you're not making them from scratch, Ty."

"I don't know why you're asking that, but no. Toaster waffles."

"Good."

"Um, why is that good?"

"Waffle irons scare me," I answered, giving my best little girl pout.

We both laughed, and I took my coffee to the table, sitting in the chair that was being bathed by the sun coming through the windows. The warmth felt great on my back.

A few minutes later, Ty brought our plates to the table and sat, the syrup dispenser in his hand. He'd already covered the waffles in melted butter, and gestured his desire to pour maple syrup on mine for me. I nodded.

It was a nice breakfast. Good food, good coffee, good company.

When we were finished eating and Ty stood to clear the table, I reached over and put my hand on his.

"Yes," I said quietly.

He looked down at me, a confused look on his face.

"Yes what?"

"I promised that when the tour was over, I'd have a decision for you, an answer."

"Are you telling me that you're going to move in?" He looked surprised.

"Yes, Ty. I just needed the time to realize—"

I didn't finish my sentence because his lips had suddenly encompassed mine, both of his hands cupping my face.

"You have no idea how happy it makes me to hear you say yes. I know all too well that it wasn't an easy decision for you." He took my hand and had me stand. "I didn't really fully explain something to you before I left, and I probably should have." We'd moved from the kitchen to the couch, his arm around my shoulders. "I already told you that, in the years since I've been touring, I've always felt conflicted when a tour ended. It was good to get home, but for me, getting home meant my cold, empty apartment in North Beach. It was always one extreme to the other – huge venues packed with screaming fans to being alone in my so-called home. A few times, just to avoid that, I stayed at my parents' place for a few days, to decompress and not be alone. "It took a long time for me to realize—"

His eyes scanned the ceiling, as if he was looking for a way to express something he'd never articulated before. "-- Too long for me to get past the superficiality of the fame and everything that came with it, to see that, while I had thousands of people who loved the star I was, I had no one to love *me*."

I felt myself starting to tear up again. He was baring his soul to me, sharing his heart.

"When I moved here, it got worse. A bigger empty house, not even what I could call a home. To be honest, I was crazy lonely. I needed that to change, so when you blasted into my life and we became lovers, I knew I had to ask you to come live with me. This time I'd have someone who did love *me* to come home to. It gave me something totally beautiful to look forward to."

I closed my watery eyes and snuggled against his chest where he couldn't see my tears.

CHAPTER 8

A few mornings later, I opened my eyes to find a chocolate cupcake with a lit candle in my face. Tyler was holding it in the palm of one hand, sitting on the edge of the bed.

"Happy Birthday, kiddo!"

I let out an exasperated huff.

"Shit! How'd you find out?" I demanded, sitting up so abruptly that he had to move the cupcake.

"I'll give you one guess."

"Nick. I'm beginning to regret that you two have become friends. Will I have no secrets?"

"Nope. Now you have both of us to contend with."

"Oh, great. Look, I appreciate the sentiment, but let's not go overboard, okay? I've never really liked birthdays."

"What? How can you say that? Birthdays are great! I mean, in my family, they've always been a really big deal! I'm following tradition here."

"My birthdays have just been a reminder of what I haven't gotten done in my life."

"My god, Phaedra! You're not even thirty yet! You're way too critical of yourself! I insist you let me make today special, and I won't take no for an answer."

So I reluctantly resigned myself to being the birthday girl. I had to remind myself that this relationship we were in was completely new to both of us, and we needed time to see what worked and what didn't.

I got dressed and headed down to the kitchen, where he'd set up a lovely breakfast on the table by the window. Multi-colored peonies from the yard were in a vase, kissed by the morning sun coming in through the diamond-pane windows.

He brought over two double espressos, and then Huevos Rancheros, hot off the stove.

"The first breakfast I ever made for you, remember?"

"It wasn't even four months ago. Of course I remember. We'd only met, what, two days before that?"

"Yeah. We really took each other by storm, didn't we? I think it was a huge surprise to both of us that it ever even happened."

"No kidding. That day we were introduced at the restaurant, I thought you were an obnoxious, self-centered rock brat."

He laughed. "Yeah, I could tell you weren't impressed by my celebrity. That actually made me like you right away."

"What? I had no idea. You always seemed to be criticizing me and pushing my buttons."

"Aw, I was just messing with you, trying to get you to loosen up so the act we needed to play would work. And I found you fascinating. Even more so now."

I had to smile. This guy had learned right from the start how to push the soft buttons that lived down deep in my psyche - buttons that had been hidden by the bigger, harder ones that made up the maya of serious toughness I'd created for myself early on in my life.

When we finished breakfast, he took my hand and headed toward the front door.

"Come with me. I have a present for you."

"Ty, that's not necessary–"

"I don't want to hear it. You will knock off this anti-birthday shit and appreciate that I want to do this for you. Stop building these walls in your head."

What could I say? He was right. I tended to build walls to protect myself from hurt and disappointment. Maybe it was baggage from my childhood, from a mother who had basically disregarded me. If it hadn't been for my father pretty much being the antithesis of that, I'd be a total mess. He challenged me to be my best self, even when he'd disapproved of my career choice, and provided humor and love up until the day he was killed.

Tyler led me out the front door, and put a hand over my eyes. We walked over toward the driveway, and he lowered his hand. There was my trusty old Toyota, looking like it badly needed a serious washing. But on the other side of it was another vehicle. He led me around the Toyota.

"Happy Birthday, love!"

I was speechless. It was a brand new Jaguar SUV, an I-Pace according to the badge on the side. It was a gorgeous British Racing Green.

"I asked Nick about the color. He suggested the green, since it was the color of the Triumph TR-3 your dad had that he said you loved riding in. Jaguar doesn't make the I-Pace in British Racing Green so I had to have them customize it, rush. I got the electric Jag so it's environmentally cool, and it's got lots of room in the back, in case you ever need to haul more bags of people's trash."

"Ty, this is too much!" I protested.

"No, it's not! Damn it, girl! Will you just accept it? I can afford it, okay? Hell, I got my mom a car for her birthday last year, and she was cool with it."

"But I–"

"Nope. Don't want to hear it." He handed me the keys. "Grab your purse. You're going to drive us up Mt. Tam."

A few minutes later, as I drove, I had to admit that the car handled the twisting road up to the parking lot near the crest of Mount Tamalpais smoothly and effortlessly. I was quickly losing my resolve to make him return it. I figured it was related to my life-long problem of accepting compliments and gifts. More mommy baggage, I guessed.

We parked and hiked up the path to the summit of the mountain. It was windy and a bit cold, but the view, as I remembered from visits with the family over the years, was 360 degrees astonishing. To the south, the city would soon be enrobed by what locals had years before dubbed Karl the Fog. To the west, we could just barely see the sun-dappled waters of the Pacific. At the foot of the mountain, not visible from our vantage point, was our Tudor.

Our Tudor. It felt odd referring to it that way.

We climbed up on the top boulder, Tyler giving me a hand up, and sat down, facing the ocean. He put an arm around my shoulder and pulled his phone from his pocket.

"Birthday selfie time!" he laughed, taking a few photos. "Y'know, I just might post one of these on my Instagram."

I pulled away from his grasp, almost slipping off the rock.

"No! You can't do that!" I exclaimed.

He looked at me, his brow furrowed.

"Why not? I don't think you're ashamed of me, or of our relationship, so what's the problem?"

"What -- what about your fans?" I stuttered, grasping for a reason. "Girls like to fantasize about their music and acting idols. And isn't that something you should run past Frank and your new management company? The PR--"

Tyler stood up abruptly and jumped off the boulder onto the dirt path. He reached up to help me down, grasping my shoulders with both hands, and looking into my eyes.

"Look. We're no longer a secret. We're together now, and I want to share my new happiness with my followers. They'll be happy for us. I know them."

I looked down at the ground, unable for some reason to meet his eyes.

"I just don't know if I'm ready for that. I'm not a public person, plus it could affect my job as an investigator–"

He let go of my shoulders, turned away for a moment, then back to face me.

"Do you really need that job? I could take care of you–"

My jaw dropped. I turned and started back down the path toward the parking lot below, stomping the dusty ground. Tyler rushed past and blocked me.

"*What the hell*?" he demanded, gesturing with his arms.

"You can't be serious!" I responded. "You'd want me to give up my work, my career? Ty, you should know me better than that!"

He let out a sigh and looked down at the dirt path.

"Damn! I keep doing this! I keep pushing you and–" He shook his lowered head. "I feel like I've fucked up your life."

That threw me for a loop.

"What are you talking about?"

"If it hadn't been for me, you would never have been dragged into all this, and you could've been doing whatever you wanted with your life."

"Ty, this isn't the first time you've tried to take on a huge burden of guilt."

"But it does boil down to me. If I hadn't been such a user of women who were willing to be used, those three wouldn't have been killed. Sarah wouldn't have had a reason to kill them. I didn't have to be like that. I let it happen."

"We've been over this before, more than once, and you just said it yourself - they were willing to be used. They wanted you to use them for sex. But if Sarah hadn't been in the picture–"

"We never would have met. Ever. That thought makes me incredibly sad."

"Me, too. But Ty, my life wasn't exactly wonderful before you came along." I reached up and ran the fingers of my left hand through his hair, looking into his eyes. "Y'know, I think that you and I are victims of kismet."

"Kismet? I don't understand. Is that good or bad?"

"It's very good. Kismet is like destiny, or—" I smiled as I turned my eyes toward the ocean, "—something that's simply meant to be."

He looked at me and smiled, those green eyes now brightened.

"Kismet. I love it." He stroked my cheek, his hand chilled by the wind, but I didn't mind. "So we're okay? I told you before that I feel we're meant to be, but I never want you to feel that I'm holding you back from your own plans and dreams. I really didn't mean to - especially today, for god's sake!"

How could I resist those green puppydog eyes, practically tearing up? They were clear green now. The gold-flecked contacts were gone along with Eros, and I preferred his eyes this way. I reached over and put my arms around his waist. He hugged my shoulders. We turned and started down the path, hand in hand.

"So, where to now, birthday girl?" he asked as he got into the passenger side of the car.

I thought for a minute as I slid in behind the wheel. The seat fit me like a glove, and I had to admit it made me feel very cool. He'd found yet another new button inside me to push.

"Y'know, I'd like to go back in time to my eighth birthday party. We're going to my favorite pizzeria in the Sunset for lunch, then maybe a little spot I used to go to when I was younger."

He chuckled, reaching over to tousle my hair.

"And where is that, may I ask?"

"No, you may not ask."

"Ooh! Mystery! Let's get going then!"

CHAPTER 9

After the pizza, I started driving westward. It was late afternoon, so the street traffic was getting heavier, but it got lighter when I turned into Golden Gate Park. I drove on until we reached the Presidio, and a parking lot Ty recognized immediately.

"Baker Beach!" he cried happily as he jumped out of the car and ran over to the cliff next to the path that would take us down to the beach.

We walked down to the sand and the shore. Only a few other people were there, drinking in the view.

"I used to come here a lot with my family growing up!" he exclaimed with the joy of a little boy. "I haven't been in ages!"

"I came here, too," I said as I looked behind us. I pointed to a house that sat on the cliff above China Beach. "That's the house Nick and I grew up in. My father would walk us down to either China Beach or Baker Beach, and watch, laughing, as the two of us

chased each other in and out of the edge of the surf—"

I choked up, and started to cry. Ty rushed over and embraced me tightly.

"What's wrong?" "I thought I could handle it by now, but I can't!" I could feel tears trailing down my cheeks. "The last time I was here with my father was a couple of days before he flew to Brazil on business. That's when he and his party were ambushed in the jungle, and I never saw him again."

He cradled my head against his chest.

"Do you want to leave?"

I stepped away and looked back at the house, then out to the ocean horizon, where the fog was already moving in.

"No. He'd want me to be able to come here. Can you take a picture of us with the bridge in the background? I'd like to put it next to the one I have of him and Nick and me in the same spot. Maybe it'll help me get past this part of the grief."

"You got it."

We walked a little further down the beach to the spot I remembered from the photograph I'd put away in a box after Dad's death. The Golden Gate Bridge was behind us, with fog now creeping underneath it. It was the classic location for an iconic San Francisco photo. We stood close together and made a heart shape with our hands as Tyler took the selfie shots. As we finished, I reached up and threw my arms around his neck, kissing his cheek.

"I wish I could have met your dad," he whispered in my ear, the whisper blending with the waves crashing next to us.

"Me, too," I said, laying my head against his shoulder. Having him there to share this was comforting. "He would have liked you, I know. Let's go home. It's getting colder and the tide's coming in."

The rest of the day was spent peacefully at home, with the two of us laughing in the kitchen as we made a valiant attempt to make our own sushi. Our California Rolls looked pretty pathetic.

"We won't be Instagramming pics of these, that's for sure," Tyler laughed as he plated them along with wasabi and ginger.

I put bowls of steaming miso soup on the table next to the rolls, sprinkled on some sliced green onions, and Ty poured warmed sake into delicate cups.

"Here's to your first birthday for us to celebrate together," he toasted, raising his cup. "Just a reminder - mine's coming up in a couple of months. I'll have high expectations."

We laughed. After we finished, he stood.

"I have one last present for you. Come with me." He took my hand and led me down the hallway. He opened the door that led down to his studio, where he sat me down behind the mixing board in the booth.

"When I give you the signal, all you need to do is hit this button here. It'll start the recording. I've got everything pre-set."

Before I could say anything, he was out of the booth and sitting at the baby grand, a boom mic above him. He signaled and I pushed the button.

He'd written me a song, beautiful and passionate. It was the most personal, most meaningful birthday present anyone had ever given me.

I could feel another new soft button being pressed inside me, deep inside my soul. How was he so good at finding these things I never knew about myself?

The next morning I awoke to find myself alone. I got dressed and headed down to the kitchen, where Tyler was sitting at the sunlit table with his laptop.

"Good morning," I said as I went over and gave him a kiss on top of his head, and stroked his chin, which was sporting a healthy growth of beard, part of his new look. I headed over to make myself an espresso.

"So what's up online that won't make me fear for the future of our planet?"

He looked up at me and gave me the cheeky smile I'd already come to know meant he'd bested me on something.

"Just checking Instagram. I've got 26,842 views so far on my post."

"You didn't!" I exclaimed, sitting down and scooting my chair closer to him. "Tell me you didn't go ahead and post that picture of us!"

"Yep. Last night after you fell asleep. Captioned it 'Celebrating my lady's birthday'. Over 3,000 comments from all over the world, and almost every last one of them totally positive. I mean, you were right that a few would be pissed off, but it literally is just a few. And I was right that love of love is more powerful."

"Well, I guess you do know your fans. You didn't post the Baker pic, did you?"" "Of course not. That one's private and no one else's business."

"I'll probably email it to Nick. Maybe at some point, all three of us will take one. You can stand in for Dad."

"I'd be honored," he said, kissing my hand. "Well, I have to tell you that, out on tour, a whole lot of fans asked about you, about whether we really were a couple, and how they were grateful you'd saved my life. They still think that's what happened, I guess. Maybe you should set up a page for yourself."

"No way! You're the celebrity in this house. Leave me out of it."

He laughed.

"Yeah, well, we'll see about that. You are a bit notorious, at least on YouTube. Didn't you know you went viral?"

"The concert videos of that night?"

He nodded.

"That's sick! Can't I ask Google and YouTube to take them down? I mean, if nothing else, they show a person being killed. I'd think that's against their rules."

"It is. The videos people in the audience posted have all been edited now to not show that part, or else they were blocked. Not like the ones Nick showed me at the hospital that day– just me singing to you, then you knocking me on my ass, and flying off the stage. It's actually pretty dramatic."

"Oh, hell."

"Okay, look at it this way. PR. Use it to demonstrate your prowess as an investigator, and your ability to react on a dime, even in cases of extreme danger. Make lemonade out of it."

He tousled my hair, which was turning out to be a favorite way of his to diffuse something he found to be too serious. The doorbell rang and he got up to answer it.

"I forgot to tell you. A couple of the guys are coming over to work on the new songs with me. Oh, gee! Here they are!" he laughed.

Since I hadn't seen any of his group members for a while, I went out and said hello. The three of them took off for the studio.

I went into the office/library and sat down at the teak desk, turning on my new Mac laptop. Sitting there, I could feel a slight vibration in the floor from the music beginning in the studio underneath me. I was glad Tyler had this new direction to focus on. He would truly come into his own now.

But I felt disconnected. I missed what I'd been doing at SIA, even the drudgery of the stake-outs. What was I doing now? Nothing. Nothing for myself.

I picked up my cell phone and dialed Anne Martino's direct number. As my boss, she could tell me what I needed to know.

"Phaedra!" she said, sounding very upbeat. "How are you doing? How's Tyler? He's back now, right?"

"Yeah, he is." I took a deep breath. Did I really want to know the answer to what I was about to ask her? "Anne, am I spinning my wheels here?"

"What do you mean?"

"Am I wasting my time thinking that I've still got a job at SIA? I mean, I'm not even getting 'watch and follows' any more. I need to know what's going on."

Now she was the one to take a deep breath.

"Things have been slow. It's been tough keeping the regular operatives busy, so the partners - not including me, I want you to know - decided that you don't need the work because of your new living situation, and you've been designated as 'On Call'. I disagreed."

"I see." What now? "I really appreciate you trying to stick up for me. I've always admired you and appreciated your willingness to mentor me. I have a lot to think about."

"Think about yourself, Phaedra. No one else, not even Tyler. Follow your instincts, even before you follow your heart. That's what I've always done."

I felt overwhelmed. After a while, I changed into my swimsuit and jumped into the pool. I just lay there on the pool float for at least 30 minutes, uncharacteristically zoned out.

Had I ever felt so conflicted?

My eyes were closed. The mid-afternoon sun was hitting the water here and there, and I was in one of those sunny spots.

Suddenly, my floating thoughts were jarred when Tyler appeared out of nowhere and dived in, sending my float wobbling and almost dumping me in.

"Relaxing, my dear?" he asked, swimming over, hands on the float. "The guys just left."

We were in the shallow end, so he was standing next to me.

"Thinking. Definitely not relaxing."

"Want to share?"

"Not really. Not yet. I have some serious decisions to make."

"I get it. Things have been pretty intense, and you've had to deal with some pretty crazy shit. But I have to tell you that sometimes I feel kind of left out."

I opened my eyes and looked at him.

"I don't mean to do that to you. It's just that my work, this career I've chosen for myself, requires a lot of focus and some independence. I'm having issues on that with my bosses at SIA, and, I guess, with you, too."

Tyler started pulling the float toward the edge of the pool. He hopped out and sat on the edge, reaching out his hand. I slipped off the float and let myself go under water, then lifted myself up to sit next to him. Our bodies sent little rivers off on the stones.

"Look, I'm in a weird place, too," he said, wiping a drop of water from my forehead. "I'm reinventing myself, hoping that my fans won't abandon me for it. And at the same time, I've put myself into the first actual relationship with a woman that I've ever had. Not necessarily good timing."

"Or maybe it _is_ good timing. So you're not facing your reinvention alone."

"I get the feeling you're working on reinventing yourself, too."

"Yeah, I think you're right. I've been made On-Call at SIA, so I feel like I'm suspended in mid-air." I forced a smile. "And I'm new to serious relationships myself."

He laughed, kicking the water.

"Well, to paraphrase Indiana Jones, we'll just have to make it up as we go along. Right?"

"Definitely," I agreed. I found it interesting that both of us had now made that movie reference since the day we were first introduced.

"I've got to fly down to L.A. tomorrow to meet with the record company people about my new direction. Should be very interesting. Want to come along?"

"I've got Nick coming up tomorrow afternoon with the last of my stuff from our locker. He can only do it then, since he'll have one of the guys from the band to help him so he doesn't undo the healing in his arm, and that's the only time Daniel can help him. Besides that, I don't think it's advisable to bring your live-in lover to a business meeting. I don't want anyone calling me your Yoko."

"Ah, I would never have thought of it that way, but I get your drift. I'll have to head to the airport around 7:30 tomorrow morning, but I'm going to fly right back after the meeting. Last thing I want to do is stay down there any longer than I have to. I hate L.A."

"Early dinner then, since you have to leave early?"

"Yeah. But let's do that after we visit my stylist in San Anselmo. It's time to get rid of this heavy metal look, and I always trust Cooper with my hair. He'll be thrilled that I'm done with this cut. And I want your input, seeing whereas you'll have to live with the result. Is that cool with you?"

"Sure." A new haircut to go with the beard? This could be very interesting. "Your car or mine?"

He laughed.

"Let's take yours. I'm really getting to like it. I just might have to trade mine in!"

We went back into the house and upstairs to change out of our swimwear. I thought about the next day, when I'd have some time to think over my career future.

CHAPTER 10

It was early afternoon the next day when the doorbell rang and I left the office to answer it. Nick stood there with his orange ace-bandage and a big smile, his keyboard player and best friend Daniel standing behind him.

"Hey, Slick!" Nick said, giving me a hug. "Tyler home?"

I waved to Daniel, who waved back.

"He had to fly down to L.A. for a meeting at the record company, to go over the game plan for his re-invention. He's anticipating blowback from them."

Nick chuckled.

"Oh, fuck them. I think it's great he's given up on that tired metal stuff. I mean, yeah, it got him to where he is now, but still."

I gestured them inside.

"Great house, Phaedra!" Daniel said, looking around. "Not what I would have expected."

"That was my first impression, too," I responded. "But I learned pretty fast that Ty was full of things I didn't expect."

The two looked at each other with arched eye-brows.

"Oh, please!" I laughed. "Before we unload the pick-up, do either of you want coffee or anything else to drink?"

"Let's just get the stuff out of the truck, and then we can relax," Nick suggested.

"Okay. There's a storage area at the back of the garage where we can stash it all."

We spent about fifteen minutes moving boxes to the storage, Daniel ogling my birthday present of the electric Jaguar as we passed it. The last item out of the truck was a trunk about three feet by two feet, faded dark green with "U.S. Army" stenciled on it many years before.

"I want this one inside," I told the guys. "It's Great Aunt Mary's, and I never checked it out when I inherited it."

Daniel picked it up and we headed back into the house. He set it on the floor next to the coffee table, and we all sat down on the couch.

I watched as Daniel seemed to give Nick some sort of signal by tipping his head toward the hallway. Nick got it and turned to face me.

"Um, do you think Tyler would mind if we showed Daniel his studio downstairs? I've told him how cool it is, so it'd be great if he could see it."

Ah, musicians!

"Sure. He'd be flattered that you're interested. Follow me."

I took them down the hall to the door that led downstairs. I turned on the red light and opened the door at the bottom.

"Welcome to what Ty calls his Den of Musical Iniquity! Just don't push any buttons."

Daniel's eyes widened and he walked slowly around the room. He was drawn to the keyboard stack, which stood next to the Baby Grand, and I almost thought I could see him drooling. I had to smile.

"So this is where he's crafting his new music?" Daniel asked. "Wow! A Bosendorfer! I've never seen one in person. They're supposed to be incredible."

His fingers hovered over the keys of the piano without touching them.

I looked over at Nick and signaled I was going to do something.

"Have a seat and give it a shot," I said, gesturing at the bench. "He'd want you to."

His mouth agape, Daniel sat on the bench seat and poised his hands over the keys, as if he didn't dare touch them.

"Just do it, dude!" Nick exclaimed, impatient as usual.

After a little further hesitation, he began to play what I recognized as one of their band's songs. He riffed on it, and got lost in the moment. Nick and I smiled at each other. His best friend was deeply in the zone.

When he finished and stood up, he thanked me for letting him experience the instrument. Then I saw him gesture to Nick that he was supposed to do something.

"Yeah, all right!" Nick said gruffly. He looked over at me, where I sat on the drum kit throne (as Nick had at one time told me the seat is called). "So, uh, do you think it would be cool if I asked Tyler about producing us?"

"You know I can't speak for him, Nick. Plus, he's focused right now on developing the new act and writing a lot. Maybe once everything's settled. But I'd still talk to him about it now anyway. Put the idea into his thought stream for later."

"Maybe you could–"

"No. I'm not getting in the middle of this. I've got a lot I need to deal with myself right now, plus you're a big boy. Pitch yourself."

"Yeah, you're right," he sighed. "We're a ways off yet to being ready for a producer, but when we are, I hope he'll do it. After all, I am your brother, and maybe his future brother-in–"

"Stop," I said, raising a hand toward him.

"Sorry, I didn't mean to–"

"Just don't, okay? You know how I feel about that."

Daniel looked at Nick with a quizzical expression.

"My sister doesn't believe in marriage. Thinks it's an unnecessary and antiquated system that subjugates the woman. Did I get that right, Gloria Steinem?"

I shot Nick a dirty look and gestured that it was time to head back upstairs.

CHAPTER 11

A few minutes later, I was alone in the house again.

I sat down on the couch and looked over the army trunk. The lock on it had long since rusted and become useless, so Mary had used heavy rope as a substitute. I struggled with untying knots that probably hadn't been undone for decades, and finally fetched a Swiss Army knife to just cut through it, not without difficulty.

I lifted the top off and leaned it against the coffee table. There was a layer of very dingy tissue, which looked delicate enough at this point that I got up and fetched a paper bag to put it into. My suspicions as to its condition bore out as pieces of it crumbled when I lifted it to the bag. Some fell to the carpet by my feet.

A garment bag was the first item. I took it out and stood to hold it up. I hesitated to open it, figuring it would probably reek of mustiness, but the plastic was still clear enough that I recognized it as some sort of uniform. A heavy leather jacket, pants and a khaki shirt. She must have been proud of her service to have kept those bulky things.

Another layer of aged tissue revealed a book - her journal. I was immediately intrigued.

In many ways, Great Aunt Mary, my father's aunt, had always been my favorite relative. She'd had a keen mind, a great wit, beautiful auburn hair all the way into her nineties, and she'd seemed to hold her great niece in high regard. That alone had endeared her to me.

I knew she'd been a librarian, and an expert in antiquarian books, but knew little else. She'd lived in Berkeley most of her adult life, and had told me stories of her research trips to Europe, studying writings from throughout history. I was enthralled, impressionable young girl that I was.

She'd provided for me the female role model I needed. My mother had always fallen far short of that.

I picked up the journal and held it, running my fingers over its aged leather bindings. It was a fairly thick book, so I figured she'd probably been writing her life into it. This was going to be fascinating reading. I opened it

'Mary Elizabeth McCaffrey.'

I'd never known her middle name. And I'd never heard her referred to by McCaffrey. It was always Johannson. Interesting, considering that, as far as I knew, she'd never married.

The first entry was from November 1943, rather late in her life to start a journal, but maybe she'd had an earlier one and this book was special. At one point, she wrote about her boyfriend, who'd just enlisted in the Army and was taking off for boot camp in a few days. She wrote about how she'd miss him and was worried for his safety, since it was inevitable that he'd be shipped to either the European or Pacific theaters - equally dangerous assignments. The entry from two days later was punctuated by lots of exclamation points. He'd proposed, and they planned to marry when he returned. Reading that, I had a sinking feeling that their decision to wait was not the right one.

After a number of entries where Mary talked about her work, her studies, and her letters to and from her fiancé (who'd been shipped to

England), I came to passages from June 1944. When I saw the date, I shuddered for a moment. As I read on, my fears were realized.

At the end of June 1944, Mary had received a letter informing her that her fiancé, Peter M. Johannson, had been killed on the beach at Normandy. There were no entries for several months. I suspected Mary was so devastated, she didn't want to write down her grief. Knowing now that his name had been Johannson, I figured she had taken his name as if they'd gotten married before he left. I sat back and took a minute to absorb what I'd read so far.

As I thought about what she'd lost of her hopes and dreams, I remembered always having had a sense of something empty inside her, an indefinable thing for a young girl to understand, but not for her older self. I felt profoundly sad for Mary and Peter, and the life they never had together.

I put the journal down on the coffee table, and picked up the next layer of tissue, adding it to the paper bag. I looked into the trunk.

I closed my eyes as I lifted up a picture frame. A classic photo of the times - a woman, young Mary I assumed, sitting at a restaurant or club table with a very good-looking young man. Peter, I presumed. They were holding hands and Mary was showing off her engagement ring.

I placed it on the table next to the journal. There was a second photo. It was Peter Johannson's official Army photo, with a message to his love written in one corner. His serious expression made me think he felt he'd never see her again. I put it next to the other picture.

A small blue velvet pouch lay on the next layer of tissue. I picked it up and opened it, emptying its contents onto my lap - Peter's dogtag. The Army had probably sent it to Mary as his fiancée, or perhaps his family had given it to her. I placed it next to the photos. Tearing up a bit, I picked up the journal again.

There were several pages where she talked about her work, now at the library at the University of California, Berkeley. A memorial had happened for Peter, with his family and a few of Mary's relatives in attendance. Peter had been buried in France.

Then an entry from mid-April 1945.

She'd been approached at work by an agent from the OSS. He was recruiting specialists to participate in the reclamation of Nazi looting, and subsequent return of those items to their rightful owners, assuming they'd survived the war. The war was rapidly coming to a close, and plans for this effort had started a few months before.

A new department had been set up - the Monuments, Fine Arts and Archives Section G-5 - and they needed all manner of experts to assist in the huge project, including specialists in books and manuscripts.

Mary wrote that she didn't immediately agree, but then decided that it could be her way of helping the war, or rather after-war effort, and that Peter would be proud of her for doing it.

Right after V-E Day and basic indoctrination by the OSS, Mary was put on a ship with a number of her new colleagues, and landed in France. It would be a couple of days before her group would be transported to their destination in either Southern Germany or Austria. They weren't told exactly where they were to be assigned.

She decided to rent a car and drive to the cemetery where Peter had been interred, but didn't go into detail.

On June 5, she and her colleagues were loaded into a transport and driven to a small town near the middle of Austria, a town called Altaussee. It was situated in a valley, surrounded by mountains and forest - beautiful, but with an odd feeling about it, she wrote.

They drove on until they reached what, from the rudimentary German she knew, had been a salt mine. The group was escorted into the largest building, which had been hastily set up as the main operations center.

They were given heavy-duty boots, thick canvas pants that looked very uncomfortable, and fleece-lined leather jackets that had been left behind by the Germans as they'd made their hasty retreat. So that was what was in the garment bag. The clothes were meant to protect against the caustic nature of the salt, which in some places in the mine made up 80 percent of the walls' material. And it was cold, typically an average 45 degrees.

Learning all of this at their indoctrination and assigning, Mary wondered if she'd made the right decision. But then she wrote of the anticipation of the adventure ahead - of discovering and saving priceless works of written art, just as her colleagues would be saving paintings and sculptures. It was exciting.

CHAPTER 12

Just then, I heard a key in the lock behind me and turned around as Tyler came in the door. He came over to the couch and put his shoulder bag on the floor, kissing me as he did it. It seemed odd not to have his hair hanging down below his shoulders any more, not that I minded that or particularly missed it. The cut Cooper and I had agreed on, lopping off about four inches, with some manly layering, and removal of the gold highlights, made him look, in my humble opinion, even sexier.

He came around the end of the couch and plopped down next to me.

"What's all this then?" he asked in his best Monty Python voice.`

"It belonged to my Great Aunt Mary, my father's aunt. I've been reading through her journal, but I haven't gotten all that far."

He reached over and picked up the photos.

"That's her and her fiancé, Peter. They got engaged just before he went into basic training and got shipped off to Europe."

He set the photos gently back on the table.

"I get the feeling there wasn't a happy ending."

"He was killed on D-Day, on the beach."

I felt myself on the edge of tearing up again.

"I always felt she carried a deep sadness, but I never knew until now what it was. She never spoke about any of it, at least not to me. Maybe to my father, but not to us kids."

"So what did she do for a living?" Tyler asked, settling back on the couch.

"Mary was a librarian and an expert in antiquarian books and manuscripts. She was recruited by the OSS–"

"Woah!" he exclaimed, jumping forward to the edge of the couch. "She was part of the MFA&A?"

I looked over at him, surprised.

"The Monuments thing? Yes. How do you know about that?"

"Well, I was a Psych Major, but a History Minor, and I loved history a lot more than psychology. Probably should have switched, but I didn't. The Monuments, Fine Arts and Archives Section G-5 is really famous! They did incredible work to find, preserve and try to return stuff to the original owners, if they'd survived the war. They even made a movie about it several years ago, the one with Clooney."

"I didn't make the connection. I've never seen the movie, but maybe we ought to find it on pay-to-view later and watch it. I'd like to get a better idea of what she was doing."

"Good idea," he said, moving closer to me. "So where are you in the journal?"

"Let's see," I said, picking up the journal and finding where I'd left off. "She just got done with orientation there at Altaussee–"

"Wait! She was assigned to Altaussee? That's the most famous of the repositories! It's the one they focus on in the movie because some of the stolen art that was considered a priority to find ended up being there! This is so cool!"

He was sounding like an excited schoolboy. It was very cute.

"So how do you want to do this?" I asked, the book on my lap.

"How about if you read it out loud, as if you're Mary writing it? I'm drawing on my History minor. You can draw on your Drama one."

I had to smile. This man was once again making me use parts of me I'd either forgotten about, or never knew I had. He was turning out to be good for me in more ways than one.

"Okay, let's see." I found the spot to begin. "First day in the mine. They've put me on the 4 a.m. to noon shift to start. People who've been here for a few days say it doesn't really matter which shift you're on, because you're underground and can't tell if the sun is out or not. I've put on my heavy clothes and boots, and put two notebooks and a few pens in the rucksack they gave me. Time to get a look at my new workplace!

"'It's now about 1 in the afternoon and I've just gotten back to the small room I'm sharing with the only other woman here at this point. She's on the noon to 8 p.m. shift, so she's in the mine now. I had a quick meal in the dining room that's been set up, and now I want to write down everything I can remember about my day while it's fresh in my mind.

"'There were two of us who would be working in our area, and we met up with our guide, George Nichols, at the opening to the mine, which was arched and had painted above it the words 'Steinberg aufgeschlagen in Jahre 1319'. I asked George if it was true that the mine had been established over six hundred years ago, and he said yes, but that it had been greatly expanded over the centuries, as demand for salt became heavy.

"'When we entered into the mine, it became dark right away, even with lights strung along the corridor. George informed us that the mine itself was 700 feet underground, and had eighteen levels that comprised 40 miles of tunnels! I couldn't believe it! Then he told us we would be heading to two rooms in what they called the Library, but that it was about 3/4 of a mile from the entrance. We couldn't use the small tram system, as it was being used to move artworks, so we started walking.

"'Now I know why the OSS people had asked if I was claustrophobic. The walls, mostly made of salt, seem very close in, so I've decided I have to train myself to ignore that.

"'When we finally got to the Library rooms and George opened the heavy door to the first room, I couldn't believe my eyes. Rows of new-looking wooden shelves, covered with crates and stacks of loose books. There are a couple of desks over against a wall, and I put my rucksack down on one of them so I could take a look around.

"'Most crates are stenciled with 'ERR', and would have ended up at the never-built Fuhrer Museum in Linz, so we're told. A few are also stenciled 'Sehr Wertvoll', which George says means 'Very Valuable'.

"'Apparently the Germans had been meticulous about their record-keeping as looted items were shipped to repositories, so a lot of what we'll be working on has good records, and will make our job easier, researching where items were taken from, grouping them, and preparing them for return to their rightful owners, if they can be found. There will be about twenty of us working in the Library once everyone arrives. But for now, there are just five of us to get started.

"'George says that the crates closest to the door in this room came to the mine in the last weeks of the war, and that so much was arriving, they couldn't keep up with the records, so shipments were just listed by the crate number and not broken down further. We're going to tackle the older, well-documented ones first, since they'll be quicker to process. The later ones will take a lot more time.

"'We don't know how long we'll have to be here. There's so much work to be done, I feel a little overwhelmed. But I'm honored to be a part of this important work, so however long it takes, we'll get it done!'"

I put the journal down and stood.

"That's made me thirsty," I said, heading toward the kitchen. "Can I get you anything?"

"Just a beer for now, but I'm hungry. How about we call out for Chinese or Thai? This is too good to stop. I can read for a while when you get tired."

While we waited for our Thai food to arrive, I continued reading. Mostly pretty dry day-by-day descriptions of the processes involved, but Ty was engrossed. The history nerd in him was in full bloom.W hen the doorbell rang and I answered the door, we decided to take a break and set up at the kitchen table. It was dark by then, so Ty decided we'd eat by candlelight.

I was finding out that he was quite the romantic, certainly more so than I was. But he was doing his best to convert me, and it was starting to work.

After finishing and cleaning up, we returned to the couch. Ty offered to read for a while.

More of the daily grind, with snippets here and there about an exciting find. The shifts now comprised ten people each, and Mary's group included one more woman, an Assistant Professor of Literature at Wesleyan. They became friends quickly.

"I'm going to hand this back to you," Ty said, smiling. "I don't think I'm cut out to do Mary's part. You do it much better."

I laughed and took the journal from him. We sat back on the couch, with pillows under our arms, and got comfortable.

Regardless of the way-less-than-acceptable working conditions and problems with supplies and transports, Mary and her colleagues were in their element and having the time of their lives. That was clear in her daily narratives. But then, a couple of weeks after her arrival, word was spread that they needed to complete their work by early July, as the Russians were threatening to advance into the area, and had been looting everywhere they could, destroying most of what they found.

Mary said that they were all motivated by the threat, but knew it was impossible to finish their work that quickly, whether it was in her library area or in paintings, sculptures, or any of the other arts. They did complete their work on the well-documented materials on time, but that left dozens of crates of books and manuscripts to be meticulously sorted through, listed and cataloged, then packed for shipment to the main collection point in Munich.There were pages and pages of Mary's daily writings. Interesting, but still a bit dry. I think we were both hoping for something more to happen.

As the saying goes, be careful what you wish for. You just might get it.

CHAPTER 13

We were up to mid-August now in Mary's journal. Work in the Library rooms was trudging along, especially since they were deep into the "miscellaneous" crates. They felt a little less pressure to rush, since the Russian threat had diminished, but the work was tedium accented by occasional exciting finds. Then things got weird.

"'Today was a bit rough, as half of my co-workers are laid up with what seems to be influenza, so we didn't get as much done as we normally would have. When it was getting close to the end of the shift, around 11:30 in the morning, my four co-workers asked if I minded sticking around for the next shift to arrive so that they could head back to their rooms. I'm hoping this influenza isn't going to stop our work in its tracks, and I certainly don't want to get sick myself.

"'So I was alone in the room for the first time. It felt a bit spooky, but I occupied myself by continuing to sort through a crate I'd started on earlier. It had hastily been stenciled with 'Sehr Wertvoll', and something I hadn't seen on any other crates - the letters FW scrawled in black paint. It was all sloppily done, unlike other crates.

"'What I'd found in it earlier hadn't been especially remarkable, and I listed each piece on the sheet on my clipboard, with a description, title if any, and any notations attached as to where and/or from whom it had been taken. Unfortunately for our work, such notations were few and far between. I found myself sighing out loud.

"'Then I reached down into the crate. My eye was caught by a heavy blanket covering something. I lifted it out carefully and carried it over to one of the desks, where a lamp would help me determine what was covered. I unfolded the blanket and found a metal box the size and shape of a fairly thick textbook. I wanted to identify and catalog it, but I couldn't see how to open it. A line runs around the middle of the spine and all around the other sides, but it's all so tight, it's like it had been hermetically sealed.

"'I'm frustrated by this setback, but also intrigued. What could be inside? And what's the meaning of the scrollwork and the symbol that's artfully molded into the metal? I can't even tell what kind of metal it is, maybe copper, but it's in remarkable condition for as old as I believe it must be.

"'What I did next, I'm ashamed to admit here. For some mysterious reason I can't explain, I unzipped my leather jacket and put the box next to my body, closing up the zipper again. The next shift was starting to arrive, and I filled them in on where my team and I had left off. I started off on my long walk to the mine entrance, feeling the box against my chest as I walked.

"'My mind was blank until I reached the entrance. That's really strange for me to feel that way, so I was even more confused. But I didn't want the guard there to find out what I'd done, so I quickly decided to feign illness, as if I too had influenza, so the guard would let me rush back to my room without checking me over. It worked.

"'As usual, my roommate is in the mine on her shift, so I'm alone now in the room. I've locked the door and unzipped my jacket. The box is now sitting on my bed, but I'm at a loss as to what to do with it, let alone why in heaven's name I've stolen it. What am I doing?

"'I'll have to hide it among my own clothes in my suitcase. I know that the right thing to do is to return it, but I can't. I don't know why, but I have to take it with me when I go back to Berkeley. It doesn't make any sense, but I have to do it.'"

Ty and I looked at each other, our eyebrows arched identically.

"Does this seem like something Mary would do?" he asked. "I mean, stealing something like that."

I shook my head.

"Not at all. At least the Mary I knew wouldn't have. She was always so totally by-the-book, pardon the expression, this seems way out of character."

"Well, she was a lot younger than when you knew her. Maybe she was, shall we say, youthfully reckless?"

"I don't think so. Something weird was going on that even she didn't understand. Maybe there'll be something more as we read on."

He nodded, and we continued reading. The rest of Mary's narrative was just more chronicling of the day-to-day work, mentioning a few specific items they'd found, but no further mention of the mysterious box.

It turned out that her work was finished in mid-September, and she was going to return home to Berkeley. The journal had no more mention of the box, or how she was going to sneak it back home. She wrote about the train ride and then the ship voyage to New York. She took a train cross-country, and got home at the end of the month.

Nothing about the box. We were actually feeling quite bummed about that. A mystery left hanging.

At that point in the journal, the pages became blank. We leafed back a bit, but nothing else had been written. But then, a few pages from the back cover, we found an envelope.

'Phaedra,' was written in what I now recognized as her meticulous script.

"What the–" Tyler said, staring at it. "Open it!"

I got up to go to the kitchen. I pulled a knife from the knife block and sliced open the top of the envelope. I didn't want to just rip it open and ruin it. I headed back to the couch, where Ty looked positively giddy with anticipation.

"It's probably an explanation of why she left her trunk to me. Let's see."

I drew the paper from the envelope and unfolded it. Her pristine script again.

"'My dearest Phaedra. Since you're reading this, obviously I have passed on. I want you to have this trunk, since its contents have been so important to me all my adult life. It helped me stay connected to my dear Peter, and reminded me what I'd done at the mine at the end of the war.

"'If you haven't already done so, remove the blanket that should still be at the bottom of the trunk.'"

Ty and I looked at each other and shrugged our shoulders in unison. Since my hands were full with the letter, Ty reached down and pulled out more aged tissue, putting it in the bag. There was another framed photo, this one looking like it was of Mary and the full complement of specialists at the Altaussee project. They all looked tired but proud.

He put the photo on the coffee table next to the others and moved back to looking into the trunk.

I watched as his face froze and almost turned pale.

"What is it?" I asked, worried.

He didn't answer. Instead, he reached into the trunk and carefully pulled back. I didn't have to ask. It was the metal box Mary had stolen from the mine's library room.

"Oh my god!" I exclaimed.

"I can't believe it!" Ty said as he laid the piece on his lap. He moved his fingers over the seam that ran around the sides, just as Mary had described.

"She did keep it!" I reached over and touched the book-shaped box.

"Why? Maybe she'll explain it."

"Back to the letter.'Yes, I kept it and brought it home with me. To this day, I can't explain why. It bothered me so much, I couldn't keep it in my apartment, so I put it in my safe deposit box at my bank. I was afraid to confess my theft to the OSS, as they would probably arrest me. I kept quiet about it and told no one what I'd done.

"'You, my dear Great Niece, are the only one who now knows what I did. I was never able to determine from whom it was appropriated, only that it was in a bulk crate that contained items from France. That's all I can tell you.

"'I've always sensed a hungry curiosity in you, Phaedra, and determination much stronger than I possess. I pass this mystery on to you now. Somehow I know you will discover its secret. But be careful. There's something about it I can't describe. Perhaps if you're able to find a way to open it, it will finally reveal its secret. But don't tell anyone. Don't go public about it. I don't know why, but I always felt like someone wanted it. Wanted it badly.

"'Good luck, my dear girl. I have faith in you. I always have.

"'Love, Aunt Mary.'"

I put the paper on my lap and lowered my head to rest on my knees. She'd loved me as much as I'd loved her. I felt Tyler's hand on my shoulder. I sat back up and his hand brushed away a tear on my cheek.

"She knew what kind of person you'd become, I think," he said, shifting the box from his lap to the couch cushion. "You'll figure this out. *We'll* figure it out, if you don't mind me tagging along."I smiled. "I wouldn't have it any other way. Let's take it into the kitchen. The light over the table will make it easier to check out detail."

CHAPTER 14

So we returned to the table by the window and turned on the light fixture that hung over it, its topaz-colored bottle-glass sending patterns onto the walls. Tyler set the box down, and we sat, just staring at it, not speaking.

"So what the hell is it?" he asked after a couple of minutes. He turned it around in a circle.

"I can't even say for sure that it's a box. It could be a book, in and of itself," I said, touching that closed seam. "But the seam goes all the way around, so that pretty much rules out it being a book. The design seems unique and intricate. And that symbol, or whatever it is–"

"I think I might know what it is," Ty said quietly, running his fingers over the large symbol in the middle of the box's top. "It could be a hallmark, a maker's mark like silversmiths have used for centuries to sort of autograph their work."

I chuckled.

"Leave it to a celebrity to equate a craftsman's mark to an autograph!"

He looked over at me with a faux hurt expression.

"Hey! I'm a craftsman, too!"

I chuckled again and reached over to pat his stubbly cheek.

"Of course you are," I said in my best mommy-encouraging-her-lit-tle-boy tone. "But how do we find out whose mark it is?"

"Well, let's Google hallmarks and maker's marks to start. That's usually a good place to find leads."

While he left to get his laptop, I looked as closely as I could at the shapes that ran along the outer edges of the top of the box, surround-ing the symbol. They reminded me of a shape I'd known about since childhood - the Cretan Spiral - a shape like a maze or labyrinth. But what would be the significance? Just fancy decoration?

Tyler came back to the kitchen, carrying my laptop.

"Mine's down in the studio, so I brought yours," he said, laying it on the table between us and opening it.

I hit the power button.While it started up, I pointed to the spirals. There were eight of them.

"I think these are Cretan Spirals. They're also found in some Celtic spots in Europe and Britain. Have you ever been to Grace Cathedral on Nob Hill?"

"Yeah, years ago when my cousin Eleanor got married there. Why?"

"They have two of the spirals in the floor, including one in the nave. It's a tradition for people to walk it. Supposedly it energizes them, or something like that. And there's one made of stones out at Land's End that an artist created. Some people call it a labyrinth. People walk that one, too. But the most famous one is in the nave of Chartres Cathedral."

"So why do you think they're on here? It looks like they've been embossed into the metal so they have depth. But the symbol in the middle is raised, like it was molded from the metal."

I ran my fingers over the center and felt its curves.

"What do you think this is?" I asked, turning the box to get a different vantage point.

It was a cross with spear-like points, and a snake coiled around it, looping its head around to face forward. At the upper tip of the cross were two wings, with a crown centered above them.

"I think it's a caduceus," Tyler said, reaching over and typing something on the keyboard.

"A what?"

"A caduceus, the symbol of Hermes or Mercury, depending on whose history you're looking at." He turned the laptop toward me. "Here it is. But it's supposed to have two snakes intertwined, and no crown thing. That would make it the physician's symbol. But this design is different, maybe unique. Hmmm."

I could tell he was intrigued.

"Let's take a couple of pictures of it and check it against a couple of websites."

He pulled his cell phone out of his back pocket and snapped a couple of shots, then sent them to both of our laptops.

"There are bound to be a few focusing on ancient and medieval symbols."

I entered the search parameter into Google, and it came up with four main possibilities. No luck on the first two, but when we keyed in "caduceus" on the third, it brought up a page with several examples.

One of the photos was a dead ringer. It was rough, as if it was a rubbing, but it was clearly the same symbol. Ty clicked on it. The description wasn't very helpful.

'Rubbing of unusual caduceus-like symbol. Origin unknown. Current location unknown.'

Then we went to the fourth website. There we found exactly what we were looking for

'Symbol attributed to 15th century alchemist Nicholas Flamel.'

Tyler's mouth hung open. I watched as he shook his head.

"That can't be! There's no way!" He reached out to run his fingers over the symbol.

"What? What's wrong?" I asked, touching his hand.

"I don't know a whole lot about him, but Flamel had a lot of crazy stories told about him after he died, especially about how he'd supposedly learned how to make a Philosopher's Stone and the Elixir of Life through alchemy–"

"Wait a minute!" I exclaimed, my left hand against my forehead. "Isn't that from 'Harry Potter'?"

Ty laughed.

"J.K.Rowling inserted Flamel into the plot because the myth revolved around him, and he ended up being the only real person in the books. But him being an alchemist was just a story, from what I remember. And he certainly wasn't immortal. He's buried in some church in France."

"France," I said, remembering what Mary had written. "So this could have belonged to him?"

"Possibly. Should we contact whoever has this site to get their input?"

I thought for a moment.

"I don't know. Mary said to be careful, that she thought someone was desperate to get hold of this thing." I touched the coppery top of the box. "We don't know who we can trust. I mean, how could this person have gotten a rubbing of a box that was in Mary's possession since 1945? Could there have been another one, or what?"

"A rubbing could have been done by the person who owned it before it was stolen by the Nazi's, and changed hands over the years."

"True." I looked back at the website. "But how did the person who has this website get it?"

"Well, specialists often have networks where they can share information. Does it say anything about a source for the picture?"

"No. No reference either."

"I think maybe we're going to have to contact this person."

"No. Mary said–"

"Maybe Mary was just paranoid because she'd stolen it. How would anyone be looking for it after all these decades?" He sounded a touch annoyed.

"I don't know," I answered defensively. "It makes me nervous."

"Why?" Ty responded, a look of consternation on his face.

"I don't know. I can't explain–"

"What is this, something genetic? I don't see what the big deal is. We contact the person to find out what, if anything, they know about this damned thing."

He was being pretty snippy all of a sudden. Was it just impatience to learn its secret?

"No," I said firmly, shaking my head. "You didn't know Mary. I did, and I trust her on this. Plus there's no rush to deal with it. We both have more important things to do."

He stood up and walked over to the refrigerator, drawing out a beer without asking if I wanted one. Okay...

"So how do you think we're going to figure this out?" he asked, standing behind his chair with his right hand on the back of it. "You got some sort of magical PI thing up your sleeve?"

His tone was one I'd never heard before from him.

"*What?*"

"Well, you're such a hotshot investigator, why don't you investigate this? The obvious path is right in your face, but you don't want to take it. So what's your plan, Sherlock?"

Well, he'd just pushed a button he shouldn't have.

"You need to back off," I said solemnly. I could feel my brow furrowing. Not a good sign. "This is my inheritance, whether Mary came by it legally or not, and I'll deal with it as I damn well choose. I was looking forward to working with you on this mystery, but not if you're going to be an asshole about it!"

That shut him up, but just for a few seconds. I felt like we were two goats butting heads. Not good, but I had to stand my ground.

"Fine. Be that way," he responded, turning and heading down the hall with his beer. "I'll be in the studio."

I laid my forehead down on the table, my left hand on the box. I guess it was inevitable that two pig-headed personalities would clash over something fairly petty. But so soon?

I sat there, trying to figure out what to do.

Apologize? Hardly. Demand one from him? Probably not likely to get it. Just go upstairs and crawl into bed, waiting to see if he'd come up? Not my style.

I went upstairs, put some things in an overnight bag, and went back to the kitchen table. I grabbed a notepad and wrote him a note.

'We both need to cool down. What we have together is way too special to ruin, so I'm going to the loft to spend the night. I'll be back in the afternoon, and we can talk about it then. P.S. I'm taking this damned box with me.'

CHAPTER 15

After startling Nick when I arrived at the loft, I explained to him that Ty and I had had a disagreement (I didn't tell him what about), and I'd decided to let us both blow off some steam overnight.

Nick seemed worried that our relationship was in danger, but I wasn't sure if his concern was for his sister or for his desire to have Tyler produce his band. Probably some of both.

I slept on the couch, since my old room was now Daniel's, and I'd insisted he not give up his bed. In the morning, I had breakfast with the guys, then packed up my overnighter, the box wrapped in my pajamas, grabbed my laptop, and headed down to the car.

As I drove across the Golden Gate Bridge, I wondered if I'd made the right decision to leave the night before. Had my stubbornness possibly jeopardized my relationship with this man who had unexpectedly come to mean so much to me? Had I again overreacted to something?

I'd find out soon. When I pulled into the driveway, I got out of the car and checked the garage. His Jag was there. I went back to the car, took out my overnighter, my laptop and my purse, let myself in the front door, and disarmed and then reset the security system. I stopped at the foot of the stairs and looked up. The bedroom door was open, and I could hear Ty's soft snoring.

I'd come to love his gentle snore over the past few months we'd been together. It was a sound of peaceful sleep, and more than once it had lulled me off to my own slumber.

I set my overnighter and purse on the floor at the end of the couch, and went into the kitchen, putting my laptop on the table. Next to my note, Ty had left one of his own.

'When I came upstairs at 3 and found your note, at first it pissed me off. But then it hit me that you were gone, and that it was because I'd been a jerk to you. I would have done the same thing in your place. I'm sorry, love. We'll talk.'

Then he'd drawn two hearts lying on their sides, their curved top lobes touching. In a sweet way, it reminded me of my own mental picture of us as two goats butting heads.

I went back to the bag in the living room and drew out the metal box, bringing it to the table. I put it next to the laptop and sat down, staring at the spirals that framed it.

I was beginning to seriously hate the damned thing.

"Whew! What time is it?" I heard Ty say sleepily as he came into the kitchen. He was still wearing his custom-made green silk Mr. Spock pajamas that I'd laughed out loud at the first time I'd seen him wearing them. His fans would have found them completely incongruous with his metal persona too, but I'd come to realize that it was just another example of his eclectic, always surprising personality.

He was barefoot, and his now-shorter hair was mussed from sleeping. How was it that he always looked so damned good, even right out of bed? I was jealous of that.

"About one."

He came over to the table and crouched next to me, putting a hand on my knee.

"I was rude to you, and there's no excuse for it. Will you forgive me?"

I brushed aside a lock of his hair that was askew from the rest.

"Maybe," I replied, giving him a sidelong look. He cocked his head, as confused as I'd meant for him to be. But he had indeed apologized, which was more than I probably would have done. "Just kidding."

I turned and lifted his face with both hands, planting a kiss on his lips, and running my hands over the new beard. Still crouched, he reached over and put both arms around my waist, resting his head on my lap. I put my arms around his shoulders.

"Oh, thank god!" he sighed, still holding onto me. "I was afraid I'd blown it."

"I wondered if I had, too."

"I guess we're both so used to being alone, it's a challenge to be together like this. It makes me a little nervous, but a good kind of nervous."

We let go of each other and he stood.

"I'm going to go upstairs and get dressed. Be back in a couple. Don't go away," he said, smiling and shaking his right index finger.

I had to chuckle as I watched his Spock-covered ass leave the kitchen, and he gave a saucy little backward kick as he rounded the corner to the stairs.

I never could have thought that I'd find a man who would excite me like this, not just sexually, but even more important, mentally. We shared a certain quirkiness, similar senses of humor, dogged stubbornness, love of good food and good music, and more. It was such a complete fluke that we'd ever even met, it still didn't seem quite real to me. Or to him, too, most likely. Maybe that was part of the problem.

But it was indeed real, a commitment, and we needed to treat it as such, and take it more seriously. With that in mind, I got up and started making him breakfast and some lunch for me. The kitchen smelled of bacon when he came back downstairs in jeans and a long sleeve purple and black striped tee shirt.

"Ah, read my mind," he said, coming to the stove and looking over my shoulder. "It's definitely a bacon kinda morning. No, make that afternoon."

He had his laptop with him and put it on the table across from mine. He sat, opened it and turned it on. He was quiet for a few minutes as he checked his email and I started to plate his breakfast.

"Interesting," he said, reaching over to touch the symbol in the middle of the box. "This had apparently been in the collection of a wealthy French Jew, but was appropriated by one of the heads of the Nazi organization Einsatzstab Reichsleiter Rosenberg." He stumbled a bit over the pronunciation. "They were the ones who looted the crap out of France in particular. That had to have been the 'ERR' Mary talked about being stenciled on crates—"

I dropped his plate down on the table none too gently, and looked at his laptop screen.

"Where did you find this out?" I asked, sitting down next to him. My BLT could wait.

He turned his head and looked outside.

"In the email reply from the guy with the website," he said quietly, as if he was hoping I didn't hear. But I did.

"What?" I exclaimed. "After what I said last night, you went ahead and contacted him? What the hell!"

"Let me explain, okay?" He faced me again, a serious expression clouding his green eyes. "I set up an email account under a pseudonym last night, and simply asked him what he knew about the symbol on his website. I said that, as a history buff, I was curious about it because it was different from the typical caduceus. That was it. I certainly didn't say anything about the box. I'm not stupid. He's the one who mentioned it being on a box, and who'd had it and who stole it."

I didn't say anything right away. At least he hadn't, to use his own term, been stupid. But he'd still disregarded what I'd told him the night before.

'Calm down', I told myself. 'Don't over-react again. Give it space. See what it is.'

"Okay. Hopefully no damage done," I said, scooting over to my own laptop. Then I remembered my sandwich and got up to get it and a bottled iced tea from the fridge. Tyler's double espresso was ready, and I brought it all over to the table. "Eat your breakfast, dude. It's getting cold."

Tyler looked up at me and smiled.

"Y'know, I think if we work backward from Mary at Altaussee, and follow the route that crate took to get there, we might have a better picture."

"Well, look at you, being all investigative," I said, hoping to lighten the atmosphere. "Am I rubbing off on you?"

"Maybe," he returned, echoing my earlier tease.

We both laughed. Good. Diffuse.

"I found some passages from a book called 'Salt Mines & Castles' by a local San Francisco man who spent a lot of time working with the MFA&A." His fingers moved on the touchpad. "Apparently, most of the stuff the Nazis stole in France was routed to, let's see, the Musee du Jeu de Paume in Paris, where they did initial cataloguing and packing for shipment. Some of the better stuff was on display so high level assholes could come and pick what they wanted for themselves. The best was set aside for Herr Hitler and for Goering, of course. And like

Mary said, the plan was to build a bigass museum in Linz, Austria in honor of Adolf, where most of what they'd stolen would be taken.

"It looks like Altaussee was the repository specifically for Linz, so it could be that this box was meant to end up there."

I got up and fetched Mary's letter from the coffee table, where we'd left it the night before. I opened it, looking for something specific.

"She said that the crate this was in had another marking on it besides 'ERR' - the initials 'FW'. I'd put money on a lot of crates having been marked with the initials of the Nazi bigwigs who'd put dibs on them. So who was 'FW'?"

Tyler had finished his breakfast and pushed the empty plate aside. He moved his laptop closer.

"I've got that book up on the screen, so let me check the index. If 'FW' was directly involved, he or she might be in here."

"Great. Want another cup?"

I picked up our plates and took his cup.

"Sure. Thanks," he said absently, obviously enjoying this new adventure and the role he could have in it.

"Aha!" he exclaimed, tapping on the laptop screen. "Here we go! Dr. Friedrich Wolffhardt. Let me scroll to the page he's on." After a minute, he looked up at me. "Apparently he was an upper mucky-muck in the ERR, and specialized in written art. He probably set that crate aside for himself, including our friend here, figuring he'd take possession of it at some point. But it says here he got re-assigned to the Russian front, where he was apparently listed as Missing in Action. Interesting."

"I wonder if he knew what it was, whose mark it was on top," I asked. "There had to have been a reason why he took that specific box, besides that it's a beautifully crafted piece. If he was a scholar of history, he might have known whose it was."

"Or he might have beaten it out of the French Jew who had it in his collection, if that guy even knew himself. I guess there's no real way of knowing for sure who knew what."

I hated to backtrack to it, but I had no choice.

"Did you get the impression the guy with the website might know more than what he told you?"

I watched his face for an expression of see-I-did-the-right-thing-af-ter-all, but there was none. He was absorbed in the moment. Good.

"Hard to say. He might," Ty answered, looking up at me. "But how do we approach him without letting him know we have it? If we give too much information, he could figure it out."

"And we don't know who he is, and if we can trust him. I mean, you never mentioned a box. He brought it up. Why? Does he identify himself anywhere on the website?"

"His name's on the email reply actually." He took a minute to bring up the window his email was open on. "John Hoffmann. He calls himself an antiquities enthusiast."

"Okay. Anything more? Where's he located?"

"The phone number he lists is New York."

"A common name in a huge city." I took a deep breath and let it out slowly and audibly. "My gut tells me to err on the side of caution, but everything else tells me he might be our only source of information."

"True. Should we craft another email and see what else he might know? Without tipping our hand, of course."

I pulled my chair over next to him and sat.

"Sure. Open a blank document and we'll put one together."

Half an hour later, we were ready to copy and paste. We'd kept it simple, just thanking him for his response and expressing curiosity as to how he'd learned about the symbol and where it had come from. Basically playing it dumb. We sent off the email reply and would just have to wait to hear back from him, assuming he'd be willing to take more time with Ty's fake persona.

At that point, we decided it was best to store the box in Tyler's safe deposit box, so, after taking more photos of it from every angle on his phone, we drove to the bank, stashed the box, then spent part of the afternoon doing some grocery shopping.

Ty seemed to really enjoy such a pedestrian task as that, since it was the first time in ages he could do something like going shopping without being recognized as the frontman of Eros. Now with his shorter hair and beard, he went about unnoticed, and seemed quite happy about it.

We were getting back in the car after loading the groceries in the trunk when Ty's phone pinged that he had a text. As he got in the driver's seat, he opened it.

"Hmmpf," he grunted as he finished, put the phone into its dash holder, and started up the engine.

"What?" I asked as I clicked my seat belt.

"The label's dropping me. They're unconvinced about my decision, and dubious as to whether I can make it work as well as I did Eros. Fine. Fuck 'em."

"Are you sure? Maybe you should talk to Frank about it. Maybe he can get them to reconsider," I offered.

"I'll talk to Frank, sure, but only to have him scope out a new label. I never liked those guys in LA anyway. They were Vic's deal, not mine."

I decided to let it go at that. It was his business, and he knew what direction he wanted to go.

We headed home to unpack the groceries. When everything was put away, Ty stopped and looked out at the back yard. The afternoon sun was on the pool, sending glimmers out with the ripples in the water.

"Y'know, let's do something else out in public. I really like being able to go out and not be recognized, but that won't last long, so let's take advantage and do something I haven't been able to do for a long time."

I was intrigued.

"Like what?" I asked, moving next to him and tilting my head onto his shoulder.

"Sausalito."

CHAPTER 16

"Really? Sausalito?"

He turned and looked me in the eyes. His were now just a beautiful, true shade of green, without the gold-flecked contacts (turned out I'd been right about that).

"So near, yet so far away," he answered, a touch wistfully. "I know it's touristy, but I lived at the north end briefly years ago, and I loved the vibe of the real town. I haven't been able to go since I became famous, and I miss it. I'd just like to walk around, check out some stores like we're tourists, and maybe have dinner at one of the restaurants over the water. What d'you think?"

I smiled. I was happy for him that he was now able to do "normal" things for a while. And, to be honest, it was making life easier for me. Up to the point that he'd cut his hair and grown a beard, we always had to be concerned about being mobbed by some of his many thousands of fans whenever we went out in public, so we hardly ever went out together. I would typically run errands alone, and use my own credit and debit cards, to keep his name private.

Ty grabbed his favorite pair of sunglasses and we got into his car, heading the few miles to our goal. We managed to find a parking spot on Caledonia Street, just off the main drag, Bridgeway, and decided we'd just stick to this street the locals had been able to pretty much hold onto for themselves.We walked hand in hand and checked out a few shops.

Then he moved me in the direction of what looked like an old auto body shop, but turned out to now be a co-op gallery of local artisans. We entered and Ty walked over to a reception desk of sorts. I followed.

"Excuse me," he said to the gray-haired, pony-tailed man sitting there. "I was wondering if Shoshannah Thomas still shows here."

The man looked up at him as if surprised that Ty knew the name of an artist.

"Yes, in a manner of speaking," the man answered. "We still have some of her pieces here on consignment for her family. Shoshannah transitioned last September. So you're familiar with her work?"

"I'm really sorry to hear about that." Ty's voice sounded defeated. "I was hoping to introduce her to my lady and have her custom-design something for her. I always loved her work, and I got to know her when I lived here in town years ago. Can we see what of hers is still here? I'd like to buy something to remember her by."

"Sure. Shoshannah would appreciate that. Right in this next room."

The man stood up and walked toward a darkened room just past the entrance. The lighting was indirect, with mini spots focused on a few showcases. A little bit of daylight from a small window kept it from being completely cave-like.

We were ushered over to a table, on top of which was a large wooden display case with a curved glass top. Very classic. Looking in, I could immediately tell that Shoshannah had been into creating fantasy pieces with fine metals and beautiful gemstones. They were gorgeous.

"I have one of her white gold dragon rings," Ty told the man quietly, almost reverently. "I bought it from her as soon as I started making money—" He caught himself from revealing too much. "From my new job." He glanced over at me. "I haven't worn it in a long time, since rings get in the way of my work, but now I think I'll get it out of the box it's been stored in and wear it again. I've missed having that little guy on my hand."

The gallery man smiled broadly, approving of this visitor.

"We need to get something for you," Ty said, looking intently into the case. "Yes! Right there! Can you get that blue and green ring out?"

"Of course."

After a minute or so fiddling with the case's lock, the man pulled out a ring and handed it to Ty, who held it by its shank and showed it to me.Why was I not surprised that it was also a dragon, but of a size to not be too ostentatious. It was done in yellow gold, and the dragon's shape wound around to grasp (or rather embrace) the wearer's finger. What was so striking, however, was that its scales were formed by tiny, baguette-cut bluish-purple and green gemstones, alternating their colors randomly. And its eyes were a brilliant shade of golden orange. Very dragon-appropriate.

"Beautiful, isn't it?" the man asked, wistfulness in his voice. "I think that was her favorite piece. She priced it pretty high, saying it was because of the materials, but I'm sure she just didn't want to see it go, she loved it so much."The scales are Tanzanite and Green Tourmaline, and the eyes are Citrines. I was always surprised that she'd used Tanzanite, since it was damned hard to get any back then because of the war they were having in Tanzania. But she got it all right, and made this beauty."

"What do you think?" Ty asked me, holding the ring about six inches from my face.

"Breathtaking. I can see why she was so proud of it," I responded, but then remembered how impulsive this guy was when it came to gifts.

Tyler smiled and looked back at the gallery guy.

"Write it up."

"Ty–" I started to protest.

He put his fingers on my lips.

"I'm buying this for Shoshannah," he said as we followed the man to his desk, "so it will belong to someone who knew her and loves her work. I'd like for you to wear it, but whether or not you do, I'm going to have it to remember her beautiful soul by."

I couldn't argue about that. The man handwrote a receipt, pulled a ring box from the drawer of his desk, and handed Tyler the paper.

Ty handed the man his American Express card, which surprised me a bit, but I suspected he figured this older gentleman wouldn't recognize his name. After running the card through the machine, the man handed it back.

"I know Shoshannah would really love that you're the one buying this piece. She spoke about you once in a while, about how proud she was of your success. This would mean a lot to her. My granddaughter is a big fan of yours, but I won't tell her you were here. I think she'd faint."

He laughed, and Tyler did also, but with a slightly sad look. They shook hands and we went through the door into the brisk Sausalito breeze.

"Would you wear it just for now, please?" Ty asked as we walked down the block. "Whatever finger it fits. Whichever one you want."

I sensed his unease about the ring placement. It wasn't an engagement ring after all, but a gift of affection for both the creator of it and me. However, I only ever wore rings on my left hand ring finger, so that's where it would feel most comfortable. I stopped and held out my left hand.

"Don't get any ideas," I said, smiling so that he hopefully wouldn't feel awkward. "This is the only finger rings work right for me."

At first he looked almost shocked, but then smiled as he took it out of the box and slipped it onto that finger. It fit as if Shoshannah had made it for me.

"This is the most beautiful thing I've ever worn," I said, staring at the gemstones as they caught the late afternoon light.

Ty pulled me into his arms and kissed me with deep affection. That's the only way I can describe how it felt. A couple of passers-by applauded.

As we walked, we decided to forego the mainstream restaurants on Bridgeway and go for something more local and low-key. Ty remembered a small French restaurant that he'd gone to often when he lived nearby, so we went there. It was a nice change of pace.

Later, as we waited for the check, Ty took my hand and turned it to look at the ring.

"I've had a thing for dragons since I was about four. That's why I bought the one from Shoshanna, especially since she'd made it for me after I told her about my childhood obsession. Then she sort of shifted her design focus to fantasy themes, so I guess I'm responsible in a way for you wearing that beauty right now. That makes it even more special."

Such a romantic I was with. That was so not like I'd ever been on my own, but I was evolving because of Ty, and I didn't mind it at all, much to my surprise.

It was dark by the time we left the restaurant and headed to the car. Back home, Ty went to his laptop, which still sat on the dining table.

"Let's see if we heard back from Hoffmann," he said, turning it on.

A couple of minutes later, he was in his email.

"Yep, here he is."

I didn't know why, but I felt an odd sense of trepidation. Was it because of Mary's warning, or just my natural bent toward suspicion?

"So what does he say?" I asked, sitting on the chair next to his.

"'The box I referred to is one of many items that were lost in the confusion at the end of the war. It's speculated that military and ancillary personnel involved in moving into Germany and Austria at that time sometimes stole pieces from repositories and estates. So it's impossible to know where items like Flamel's box ended up, unless they eventually appear on the black market. I've found that item to be fascinating, so I've kept my eyes open over the years, hoping it would surface, but nothing as yet. I had hoped that putting the rubbing on my website might bring a lead, but you are the only person who's inquired about it at all.

"Should you ever hear anything about it, please do let me know. We seem to share an interest in such esoterica.'"

"Seems innocent enough," Ty said, looking over at me.

"Yeah, doesn't it," I responded. I found myself moving my left hand to cover my chin and mouth. It was a gesture I typically make when contemplating something bothersome. "There's more to this than meets the proverbial eye. Something's not quite right, but I don't know what it is. Yet."

Ty took a deep breath.

"Okay, I'm not getting on your case again - believe me, I don't want to repeat last night - but why can't this just be a straightforward reply to our question? What's to be suspicious about? Please. I just want to understand where you're coming from."

"No, I know," I told him. I tapped my fingers on the tabletop. "Look, I've always been what my mother called 'a leery person'. She considered it to be a really annoying trait, but my father said it was the mark of a cautious and inquiring mind. He even showed me in the dictionary that 'leery' meant 'wary due to realistic suspicions'. So after that, whenever my mother called me leery, I took it as an unintentional compliment."

Ty laughed.

"I've said it before, but I wish I could have met your dad. I'm so glad he was there to support and encourage you, otherwise we wouldn't be here right now, together."

He reached up, turned my chin toward him, and gave me a quick kiss.

"But what about your mother? Do you think you'll ever see her again?"

I sighed.

"I don't know. I doubt it. I seriously lit into her after Dad was killed, about how she was just going to sell the house we grew up in and pack off to live with her sister, leaving Nick and me to fend for ourselves. Fortunately, we were old enough to be able to get by with the trust funds Dad had set up for us. But I couldn't then and still don't forgive her for abandoning us as if we'd never existed. She does send birthday and Christmas cards to Nick, though."

"Damn," Ty said quietly. "It's bad enough to act like she does, but to send cards to just one of her children and ignore the other is just... well, being a bitch. I've never quite realized until I met you how totally lucky I am to have the parents I have. I'm sorry you've had to go through that crap with your mother."

"Well, it is what it is, and I doubt it's ever going to change." I forced a smile. "But now, if I need some motherly input, I've got your mom to fill the gap."

Ty smiled, too.

"You know she's crazy about you, don't you? She thinks you're the perfect person to keep me in line. When she said that to me, I told her I wasn't even aware that I was out of line. We both laughed."

I got up, grabbed a couple of wine glasses from the cabinet, un-corked a bottle of my favorite Old Vine Zin, and brought it all to the table.

"Back to our Hoffmann situation," I said as I poured. "Before we go any further with this box deal, I need to find out whatever I can about him. Forward me his emails. I'm going to go into the office on Monday and use SIA's resources. They've got stuff I can't have on my own, so I should be able to dig deep into who he is. In the meantime, no more communications with him until I give the go ahead. Got it?"

"Yes, ma'am." He lifted his glass for us to toast. We clinked glasses. "Not gonna make that mistake again. I promise."

"Good," I responded, taking a healthy sip of the Zin.

CHAPTER 17

It felt oddly pleasant to walk into the SIA offices late Monday morning. I even put up with the sickly sweet greeting from Alice, the dipsy receptionist, on my way to my desk, wondering as I went if I even still had a desk to call my own.

I got high fives and waves from staffers and operatives as I passed, and even got ignored by Fuentes as he watched me walk by his office. I needed to check in with Anne Martino, my boss and one of the agency partners, to get her permission to utilize company assets for personal reasons. She could easily deny my request.

I knocked on the frame of her open door, and she looked up, smiling.

"Phaedra! So good to see you! You look great! How's not-married life treating you?"

I nodded my head. I'd mind that question from anyone but her.

"Fine. A bit boring not working, but otherwise good." I sat on the chair opposite her. "I have a favor to ask, and I'm not sure it's a kosher one."

"Ask away." She put her elbows on the desk and rested her chin on her interlocked fingers.

"I need to get deep info on someone, and I'd like to use SIA's resources to get it."

"I see. Knowing you, you wouldn't be asking this if it wasn't something you're really concerned about. Am I right?"

"Of course you are," I answered, scooting forward on the chair. "This is someone I need to know as much about as possible before we trust him with a sensitive issue. I've got this nagging feeling about him that I need to either validate or disprove. It'll drive me crazy until I can do that."

"I know the feeling. Believe me I do." She lowered her arms to the desk. "You've got my permission to use whatever you need, and I'd recommend getting Hawk's input on it."

That was easier than I'd anticipated. I appreciated her understanding.

I got up, waved goodbye, and headed down the hall to the IT room. I opened the door and immediately saw Hawk seated at his oversized desk, huddled over a keyboard. His long black hair was in a single braid almost to his waist, and he wore his requisite denim shirt, as usual.

Hawk was a full-blood Cherokee, with a Master's in Computer Science, and a head full of brilliant ways to research, capture, analyze and utilize information of all types, especially about people. I was very glad he was in.

"Hey there, Hawk," I said, not too loud so as not to disturb or startle him from his concentration.

He turned and smiled broadly.

"McCaffrey! Long time, no see! What's up?"

"I need your help checking up on someone. I need to make sure he's above board before Tyler and I have dealings with him."

"So you have doubts obviously."

"Yep. How do you recommend I start? All I have is his name and New York phone number."

Hawk chuckled.

"Hell, that's more than I've had in some cases. Let me set you up with a database we use a lot that's not available to the general public. That should give you enough info to get going on."

"Great! Thanks!"

He got up and took me over to a small desk in the corner, with a desktop computer and printer. It was old school compared to most of the equipment in that room, but sometimes that's all you need.

He sat down, turned it on, and set up the app he told me about.

"Start with this," he said as he stood and gestured for me to sit. "Once you have something, go to this other app here. It connects to government records like military service, immigration and naturalization, criminal records, etc. If you need anything else, just let me know."

"You're the best," I said, looking up at his face with its high cheekbones and icy blue eyes. When I first met him, I found him fascinating and seriously attractive, but never did anything about it. Now, looking at him, I wondered why I hadn't. Oh well..."

Indeed I am," he responded, laughing and patting my shoulder as he retreated back to his desk.

I won't go into the boring details of how I came upon the information I found on Hoffmann, but what I discovered was that he was founder and President/CEO of a company called Cyber Protection Services in Manhattan. Interesting. And he had emigrated to the United States from Germany at the age of twenty to attend Harvard, achieving a Ph.D in Economics. He became a naturalized citizen several years later.

I went into the other app to see what the naturalization information could tell me. After plowing through a lot of boilerplate, I found his record. It showed John Frederick Hoffmann, born March 14, 1944 in Munich; mother Beatriz Leyser; adoptive father August Hoffmann.

Adoptive father? What about his birth father? That seemed strange to me.

"Hawk, could you take a look at this?" I called out.

He got up and came over.

"What you got?"

"Is it common to list an adoptive father on citizenship papers, and not the birth father?"

"Common if the birth father was unknown or unclear. Let's see, yeah, he was born during the war, and there were a lot of illegitimate births happening. That may be it. But just to be sure, I can put you into the legal and vital statistics files for Germany, both East and West, and you can track down his adoption there. If his birth father was known, it should come up."

"Thanks!" I said as he entered the URL and got the site up on screen. He even got it into translate mode. It took about ten minutes for me to hone in on the adoption, by way of his mother's name, and I finally had the information up on the screen.

Fortunately, the adoption file did list the birth father's name, but I wasn't prepared for what it was.

Friedrich Wolffhardt.

I was stunned, my left hand covering my mouth. What exactly did this mean? That John Hoffmann was actually Johann Wolffhardt? I didn't like it. It felt bad, possibly really bad.

"Hawk, I need your help again," I called out.

He came over.

"Now I'm really concerned about who this man is. He owns a company in Manhattan. Maybe you can tell me something about it."

I brought up the screen that showed Hoffmann's company name.

"Oh, shit," he said quietly, crouching next to my chair. "This is the guy you're dealing with? Who's CEO of Cyber Protection Services?"

That didn't sound good.

"Uh, yes. Why?"

"Let me ask you a question. Have either of you communicated with him by email or text?"

"Tyler did, by a phony email address."

Hawk chuckled sarcastically.

"People think that's all they have to do to be anonymous. Wrong. Phaedra, if this guy wanted to, he could hack right past that phony email in a shot, and get the truth as to who sent it."

"What? How?"

"With the resources his company has, they can just as easily invade as they can protect. It's just natural, the way technology is. If he wanted, he could easily hack into Tyler's computer and look for whatever he wanted that might be on there."

"Oh, crap!" I exclaimed, thinking about what was there.

"Look, does this guy want something you have info on in Tyler's computer?"

"Unfortunately, yes."

"Then he knows. Photos?"

"Yes."

"You're screwed. He's got 'em. Do you have copies of those emails back and forth so I can see if I can detect if I'm right?"

I nodded and pulled out my laptop from my bag. A few minutes later, Hawk was looking intently at the email forwardings.

"Sorry. I can see it. He's got you guys, and more than likely, he's got your address, too."

"Oh, my god!"

I jumped up, grabbed the laptop and closed it, picked up my purse and headed for the door.

"I can't thank you enough, Hawk."

"Hey, is this guy dangerous or something? Do you want me to call the cops?"

"No, don't. I need to find out exactly what he's up to. I'll let you know what happens."

I rushed down to my car and called Ty's cell before I even started the engine.

"Hey, kiddo," he answered right away. "What's up?"

"Hoffmann's a bad guy, Ty. He owns a cyber security company, and Hawk says he hacked into your laptop through the emails. He saw the photos. He knows we have the box–"

I heard the doorbell ring.

"Don't answer–" I began, but he'd already put the phone down and I could hear him open the door without even questioning who was there. Why the hell would he do that? Damn it!

"Hello, Mr. Powell," I heard a man's distinguished voice say. "I'm John Hoffmann."

CHAPTER 18

It felt like my heart had stopped. I wanted to scream, but it would have let Hoffmann know I was on an open cell line and could hear him. My instinct told me not to give him the benefit of the doubt as to how innocent his appearance was, so I needed to scope out the situation before I did anything definitive.

I drove up to Mill Valley as fast as I could without endangering anyone else or my driver's license. I strained to hear what was going on at home as I drove, but they were too far away from the phone to hear actual words. The frustration was making me a hell of a lot more anxious.

As I reached our street, I parked about fifty feet away from the house, grabbed my shoulder purse and headed up the driveway, staying close to the trees and bushes on its far side, hoping to not be seen.

I needed to do reconnaissance before I confronted the man, so I unlocked the hidden side gate and walked around to the kitchen door, ducking low in case Hoffmann looked that way. I quietly unlocked the door and slipped in, using the fireplace wall that separated the kitchen from the living room as a shield.

I could hear Hoffmann's voice in the living room. Fortunately, the glass front of the built-in microwave was reflecting nicely, and I could see Ty sitting on the couch, his back to Hoffmann, who was several feet away near the front door, pacing. I sensed nervous agitation in him not dissimilar to my own.

I slipped back outside and around to the front of the house. I stood there for a couple of minutes, waiting for my heartbeat to calm down enough for my brain to function as I needed it to. For now I needed to act as if nothing was out of the ordinary and I was just getting home.

I took a deep breath and put my key into the lock, turning the knob and opening the door. As I stepped in, Hoffmann turned to face me, about five feet away.

"You must be Ms. McCaffrey," he said, smiling. "A pleasure to meet you. I'm John–"

"I know who you are," I said with as much steadiness as I could muster under the unknown circumstances. "Actually, I know who you really are. And I know who your father was."

Ty looked at me, concern on his face. I could now see that his hands were tied behind his back. That changed the dynamic immediately.

"Indeed," Hoffmann said matter-of-factly, reaching into his jacket.

He pulled out a small caliber gun and pointed it at my chest. Ty lunged forward on the couch, but I motioned him to stop and sit back quietly. I needed to have as much control over the situation as I possibly could.

"You found out who and where we were," I said, looking him in the eye. "And I found out that your father was Friedrich Wolffhardt."

I glanced over to see the shocked expression on Ty's face.

"My father was a great man, a great scholar."

"Is that why you changed your name?"

I saw a twitch on his face.

'Careful, Phaedra. Don't push him too hard.'

"It had to be done, to survive in post-war Germany. The name Wolffhardt had become...a liability."

"I can imagine why. He stole from innocent people–"

"No!"

The gun shook in his hand. Tyler reacted by lunging forward on the couch again. The gun was pointed at him for a moment, so I didn't dare attack. But how to diffuse the situation?

"John, listen to me. The box is just a historical piece. There's no manual inside it on making the Philosopher's Stone or the Elixir of Life. There never was. There's no such thing. It's all a myth–"

"You're wrong! My father told me it was real, and that it was in that box! He said that was why it was so difficult to learn the secret of opening it. When he recognized what it was at the Jewish man's estate, he made sure it was put in the crate he'd painted his initials on. The plan was that it would be delivered to our home after it was taken to Altaussee. But his superiors became annoyed at my father's complaints about the Linz Museum, and transferred him to the Eastern front. He arranged to become MIA, and secretly returned home, where we hid him until the post-war situation normalized enough.

"He changed his appearance as best he could, took on a different name, August Hoffmann, and married my mother under his new persona."

"And adopted you so that you'd have Hoffmann as a last name instead of Wolffhardt," I added, looking over at Tyler. I could see his chest heaving with the heavy breathing of fear

"He tried to find out what had happened to his crate at Altaussee, and was dismayed when he found that the Americans had removed everything and returned much of it to those who had owned them. He traveled to France, to the estate of the Jewish man, but it was empty, as the man and his family had been killed toward the end of the war.

"My father managed to get a job at an office that held records of the reparations, and surreptitiously found the file containing the record of his crate. The file listed all of the contents and their details. But the box was not listed. He did find a list of the names of those who had been on the team handling the books and manuscripts, and made note of all of them so he could track down whoever had taken it."

I looked over at Tyler and mouthed 'Mary'. Perhaps her paranoia about the box wasn't paranoia after all. Maybe her informal name change had been made to hide her from whomever she sensed wanted the box. There would be no legal record to link her to the 'Mary McCaffrey' Wolffhardt would have been looking for.

"He became very upset that he couldn't find the box where Flamel put 'The Book of Abramelin'. He had come so close to possessing the formula for The Philosopher's Stone–"

"Your father was wrong," I said firmly, again looking him in the eyes.

"No!" he cried out, pointing the gun at my face.

"Phaedra!" Tyler called out, jumping to his feet.

I waved him down, mouthing to him to sit and be quiet.

"My father knew! He told me on his deathbed everything he knew about the box. He made me swear at his bedside that I would find it and uncover its secrets on his behalf. The box was his–"

"No, it wasn't!" I spoke out more boldly than I probably should have, considering the gun was still pointed at my face. "Haven't you ever researched Flamel? He was just a scribe, a printer, and because of his wife's money, a philanthropist of some notoriety. The Stone myth was debunked long ago, along with the story of him being an alchemist–"

"Lies! Lies to keep me from finding it!"

"John, listen to yourself," I said calmly, in my best soothing voice. I had to bring him down a whole lot of notches, and quickly. "You've been blinded by your father's obsession. He made it yours, and you feel duty-bound to honor your oath to him. But he was wrong about the box. Let go of it. Don't ruin the rest of your life for a myth."

His shoulders drooped and his face softened into what looked like sorrow. Had I maneuvered him into a turning point? I needed an epiphany for him.

"Give me the gun, John. Please. You have an incredibly successful business and a family. Think of that. Think of what you've built for yourself completely apart from the Flamel myth, and how much all of that and your loved ones mean to you. That's what's important."

Tyler stood again, slowly this time, his tied hands making his move a bit shaky.

"She's right, John. Aren't your family and your company what are most important to you? They rely on you, and you on them. Don't throw that away."

Interesting. In the clutch, we were both using our psychology schooling to diffuse a potentially deadly situation. What a team!

I took a deep breath and slowly held out my right hand.

"Please hand me the gun, John. I promise that if you do, we won't have you arrested for what you're doing, and you can return to your family."

Tyler looked over at me and nodded his head.

"John, let's change all of this into something positive," he said, mimicking my soothing tone.

"What do you mean?" Hoffmann asked, his voice cracking with emotion.

"Flamel's box doesn't contain Abramelin's book, but it's still an amazing historical piece," Ty said with a positive aspect to his voice. "We can team up to find out what it really is and how to open it. You have the technology and expertise, and we have the box."

We both held our breath.

Hoffmann fell to his knees, turned the gun around in his hand and handed it to me. His now free hands covered his face.

As I took it, I saw that the safety was still on. He either knew nothing about how to use a gun, or he'd never intended to shoot us.

I tucked it in my waistband and rushed over to get the cord off of Tyler's wrists.

He hopped over the back of the couch and took me tightly in his arms.

"I must apologize deeply to you both," John said quietly, lowering his hands. I could see tears. His arms hung limp at his side. "You're right. My father was such a commanding, overwhelming force in my youth, I let him pull me into his obsession, and I didn't dare let it go, even though he was dead.

"For many years, the box was just a distant thought. I was building my business, got married and started a family - I have grandchildren now, by the way - and I've been very happy.But when I got that email about the Flamel symbol, it triggered that damned oath in my psyche and I was compelled to move on it. I used my company's tracking capabilities to trace your phony email account to you, Mr. Powell, and to get your address as well. It's easier to do than most people realize. You couldn't hide from me.

"I had no intention of hurting you. I just wanted to intimidate you into giving me the box that I knew you had.

"Again, I'm genuinely sorry for what I did, and I appreciate your understanding, and willingness to not press charges. Now I can return to what I truly cherish. The obsession is gone, and I thank you for that."

Ty stepped over and offered Hoffmann his hand to help the older man up, smiling. Hoffmann smiled back weakly. I sensed both weariness and relief in him.

Considering what had just happened, it was somewhat bizarre that we invited Hoffmann to sit at the kitchen table with us. I made coffee and brought the mugs to the table, along with cream and sugar. Hoffmann drank his black.

At first, we all just sat there, not knowing what to say.

"I must say I'm impressed that you were able to discover my birth identity, Ms. McCaffrey," Hoffmann finally said, taking his last sip of coffee. "And so quickly."

"It's my job. I'm a private investigator," I responded, looking him in the eye. I no longer had that sense of trepidation about him. "And please, call me Phaedra."

"Tyler," Ty added.

First name bases were in order if we were indeed going to collaborate in solving the Flamel Box Mystery.

Hoffmann gave a light chuckle.

"Perhaps it's appropriate that a private investigator brought this to an end. I'd always blinded myself to the truth because my father had been so sure of himself, and had been so determined to make me swear to him that I'd find the box and its secrets. I should have known better. I'm a man with a reputation for logic and integrity, but his obsession possessed my subconscious and bypassed all reasoning when your email arrived.

"I feel ashamed that I wasn't able to control it. And to point a gun at you both." He raised his hands to cover his face, his fingertips resting on his forehead. After a moment, he lowered them to the table. "I'm very grateful for your kindness under the circumstances. What can I do to return the gesture?"

Ty and I looked at each other, remembering what Ty had suggested in the heat of the moment. Hoffmann must have forgotten it, given that same moment.

"We're suggesting a collaboration," Ty said, sipping his coffee. "We use the resources your company has to literally unlock the box's secret."

Hoffmann looked deep in thought for a moment.

"I saw in the photos you took of the box that there's a seam that runs around its perimeter."

"Yes," I responded. "But it seems like it's sealed somehow, with no visible lock or release. When I first looked at the box, I wondered what the spirals were for, other than decoration. Could they be–"

"The literal key to unlocking it?" He smiled. "Let's find out...together."

CHAPTER 19

A few days later, Ty and I stepped off the flight from SFO to Kennedy. We Uber'd to the hotel, picking up the package we'd sent Fedex Overnight as we checked in. We had the manager lock it in the hotel safe. The package contained the Box of Mystery. We'd decided right away that we couldn't take it with us on the flight, considering TSA security and all, so it made sense to ship it to New York.

It was already after 7 pm at that point, so we decided to have dinner at a restaurant Ty had eaten at on one of his first tours. It was an out-of-the-way, small Moroccan place, with floor seating and live music. We spent the next two hours having a ball eating with our fingers and interacting with the musicians. Ty even acquiesced to playing the guitar-like instrument its player had handed to him, apparently sensing somehow that Ty would be able to play it.

Excellent musician that he is, he was able to step right into their Moroccan groove, and they all played their hearts out for what had to have been at least half an hour. Sitting back down, Ty was exhilarated.

"Man, that felt good!" he exclaimed, taking a big gulp of water. "I've got to get back into it, seriously. No more experimentation. I've just got to make a decision and do it!"

I smiled. He'd been feeling a bit lost since shutting down Eros. He wouldn't admit that he missed it all, but it was obvious to me that he did. He'd been working hard on the new music, and had my support in putting his new direction into gear. Whatever I could do to help.

After a dessert that reminded me of Baklava, we headed back to the hotel. The box-in-a-box was safely stashed in the hotel's safe, where we'd pick it up in the morning on our way to Cyber Protection Services, to meet with John.

When we walked through the front door and into the lobby of the skyscraper that housed Cyber Protection Services, Hoffmann was waiting for us by the security desk. He came over and shook our hands, smiling.

"Good to see you both again," he said, gesturing toward the elevator. We followed his lead. "I see you've brought our mystery with you."

Ty was holding the Fedex box and patted the top of it.

"A mystery hopefully soon to be solved," Ty said, gesturing for me to enter the elevator before him.

We rode quietly up to the thirty-first floor. I had a sense of heavy anticipation I was sure we were all sharing at that moment. Ty even seemed to have forgotten about his dislike for skyscrapers.

The door opened to your typical corporate lobby, replete with reception desk and leather chairs. We walked past all that and down the hall to what was obviously John's office.

He indicated we should sit on the small couch to one side of the room, he himself sitting on a chair facing us. There was a coffee table between us, and Ty set the box down on it. John stood up, went over to his desk and came back with a box cutter. I found it interesting that a CEO would have a box cutter in his desk.

I thought that he'd slice the tape himself, but he handed the tool to me. Was it because the box technically belonged to me, or was it a gesture of respect? Did it matter?

I cut through the tape and opened the top of the box, reaching in. I lifted Flamel's box out, removed it from its bubble wrap packing, and set it on the table.

John reached out and ran his finger along the seam, much as Ty had done that fateful night we'd discovered it in Mary's trunk. Then he leaned down to examine the spiral shapes.

"Do you mind if I pick it up to take a closer look?" he asked.

"Please do," I answered.

He lifted it almost reverently, turning it to see all sides, then traced the path of one of the spirals with a fingertip. He lowered the box to his lap, closed his eyes and shook his head slightly.

"I suppose you could say that I'm actually fulfilling my oath to my father now. I've held the box in my hands, and shortly we should be able to discover how to open it and what it actually contains. Regardless of what we find, I can't help but think about the damned obsession he wore like some twisted badge of honor. For me, it's been an albatross lurking in the back of my mind, and I'm looking forward to freeing that bloody bird once and for all."

Ty and I smiled at each other.

"Well, let's take this down to the lab and see what technology can tell us," John said, standing and gesturing toward the door, the box in his hands.

I felt that it was appropriate now for him to carry it.

We walked together a couple of hundred feet down the hall to double doors. John opened them with his free hand and gestured for us to enter. It was a large room, full of impressive-looking equipment, including what looked like a small CAT-scan machine. Maybe that's what we'd be using to unlock the box's secret.

A woman in a lab coat came over to us. John gave her a nod ."So this is it?" she asked as John handed it to her. Obviously he had briefed her on the mystery, as she was probably the lead in that department. "I see what you were saying about no visible opening, lock or release. Let's take a look."

We followed her over to the machine I'd speculated to be our tool, and watched as she placed the box onto the belt. Moving to the side, she pressed the button that took the box inside. John indicated we should step over to a large screen desktop computer that was obviously connected to the scanner. It was amazing to me how it was quickly able to scan past the metal of the box and show, like an x-ray, what was inside.

Papers. Not a book, but what looked like a stack of papers and envelopes, as best we could tell. Interesting. I knew we were all wondering what they would be about.

The woman, Dr. Melinda Armstrong by her badge, made an adjustment on the machine, which seemed to back up the scanner ever so slightly so that we could see the spirals and the caduceus clearly. John and Ty leaned in close to the screen.

"Do you see that?" Ty asked, as he moved his finger between two of the spirals.

"Yes," John answered, looking even closer. "They're connected. Melinda, would you look at this, please?"

She stepped over and looked closely at the image.

"You're right. There are pathways connecting them in a pattern. I'll run this through the system to find out exactly how to progress. I think you're all correct that this is a mechanism to unlock the box. What time period did you say this is from, John?"

"Sometime in the early fifteenth century, it seems."

"Whew!" Armstrong exclaimed, shaking her head. "If that's indeed true, this is incredibly advanced for six centuries ago. If you all approve, I want to document the steps we take to attempt opening it. This is something that needs to be preserved and studied, if it works as it looks like it should."

We watched as she transferred the scan to what was apparently a main computer, and keyed in instructions.

"This shouldn't take long," she said, moving over to another station to await the result. "I'm hoping it will be able to detect the path among all the connecting lines that will result in unlocking. Fingers crossed, guys. After such a long period of time, it's possible the true pathway might have deteriorated. We'll see."

About eight minutes later, a printout emerged, and Armstrong handed it to John.

"It's highlighted the lines that it detected connect both the spirals and the symbol in the center. Whoever designed and created this was careful not to make it an easy pattern. It would have taken a lot of trial and error to figure this out manually. But this should be it."

The three of us looked at each other. It was one of those moments in life where you're caught in a Vortex of Wow. That's the only way I can think of to describe what I, at least, was feeling.

This was it.

John handed me the paper.

"This is yours to do. Your aunt, unbeknownst to her, saved this for us to have here and now. She left it for you to solve, and now you can. Melinda, what can she use to follow the path?"

She stepped over to a toolbox, and came back with what looked like a copper ice pick with a wooden handle.

"I could be wrong, but I think that using copper to trace the lines might just be an additional trick here. The connecting lines are just below the copper surface of the box. It all looks continuous, from the beginning wing to the last spiral. The readout will tell you how to move."

Ty lifted the box from the scanner and brought it over to a table in the center of the lab. We all stood around it.

"It might help if I mark the spirals with numbers," Armstrong said as she pulled a pen from her lab coat pocket. She had me put the sheet down on the table and marked them.

I suddenly felt very nervous, or was it just crazy anticipation? I took a deep breath and moved the box closer to me.

"Ty, would you tell me where to go with this? I want to keep my eyes on what I'm doing."

"You got it. Steady as you go."

I smiled at him and took another deep breath. Armstrong reached over and pointed to the wing to the left of a spiral on the paper marked '1'. She then pointed to the corresponding spiral on the box itself, which was close to me. I turned the box so that it matched the printout.

"There's a very tiny dot at the tip of the right-hand wing next to Spiral 1, which tells us that that's the starting point," Armstrong said, both hands on the table.

"Okay. Ready?" Ty asked, taking a deep breath himself.

I picked up the copper stick and held it over the wing's tip.

"Put it on that dot, then pull it carefully to the middle post of Spiral 1, the one that sticks straight down," Ty instructed. I did that, slowly, trying as best I could to keep my hand from shaking. He glanced over at Armstrong to see if she agreed that I wasn't to actually trace into that spiral. She nodded.

"Now go down at an angle to the tip of the cross point and touch it. Then angle down to the middle post of Spiral 2 and touch."

I don't know if I'd ever been so intensely focused on anything in my life as I was on that damned box. It was all I could do to keep my hand steady.

Ty continued, tracing his finger along the path on the paper.

"Angle down to the center post of Number 3," he instructed, pausing to let me catch up, since I was taking it very slow. "Now up to the bottom tip of the caduceus. Okay, now angle down to the center post of Number 4. Good job. Now up to the center post of 5. Steady. Go to the left tip of the caduceus, then up to the center post of 6. Go up to touch the tip of the left-hand wing. Now up to 7's center post

."Almost there, love. Angle down to the middle of the crown. Great. Now you're going to angle up to Spiral 8-- No, wait! This is different! Don't touch the center post! Touch the one that's at the right outside. Now you have to follow it around until you get to the end in the middle, where you see the dot."

I carefully did that. I moved along the path.

"No! Don't turn there! Keep going straight!"

He startled me so much, I almost lifted the copper stick off of the surface. I looked up at Ty and gave him a dirty look, which I immediately regretted. We were all on edge.

"Sorry," he said quietly. "Follow the line now, and you're almost there."

I took a deep breath as the copper stick approached that telltale dot, and I slowly and carefully followed the indented path toward that point.

I could hear everyone else also take a deep breath as I reached the end of the pathway and pressed down on the dot ever so lightly with the copper stick, lifting it up and away from the box.

Nothing.

"*What?*" I exclaimed, throwing the stick on the table.

"Wait," John said quietly. "It's been centuries since this was last open."

As he finished, we heard a faint sound come from the box, and watched as the seam around it separated slightly.

"Yes!" Ty screamed, grabbing me into his arms.

I was speechless and shaking, which surprised me. It takes a lot to discombobulate me.

"John, you do it," I said, looking over at him. "I don't think I can."

"I'd be honored."

He reached down and grasped two sides of the box, gently lifting up. The top seemed to be on small hinges that allowed it to be raised but not removed.

"Melinda, are you getting all this?" he asked.

She had her cell phone out and had been capturing it all.

"Yes, and the lab cameras will get it, too."

"Go in close and get what's inside before I take it out, okay?"

She did so, John carefully reaching in between the hinges, and lifting out a stack of envelopes and loose papers, setting them gently down on the table. Armstrong took footage.

I moved closer and picked up the top envelope.

In lovely handwriting were penned the words "Ma Cherie Perenelle". I lifted up the next envelope, which was addressed in a more feminine hand "Mon Cher Nicolas".

I examined the rest of the stack, the others around me waiting for some word of what this was. Finishing the last loose sheet, I straightened up and looked at them.

"Near as I can tell by way of my rusty high school French, these are all love letters between Flamel and his wife. Correspondence between lovers. Nothing more."

Hoffmann silently turned, walked over to the door, opened it and walked out into the hallway, leaving the door open. Ty and I looked at each other, and he shrugged his shoulders.

I headed out the door and found John standing a few feet away, arms crossed in front of him, his head lowered.

"John, are you alright?" I asked quietly.

"For the moment, no," he responded, raising his head to look at me. "In my mind's eye, I'm seeing my father, close to death, speaking so passionately about the book he was certain was in that box. I remember it as if it was just yesterday. Now, seeing what's actually there, I feel a profound sadness for him, that his obsession was indeed nothing but a myth, just as you told me a few days ago in your home. But I also feel release. It's over. Thank God."

I stepped over and took his hands in mine. I've never been a touchy-feely person except with those very close to me, but I felt compelled to offer this man support in the moment.

"Thank you," he whispered, smiling.

Tyler came out into the hallway and walked over to us, the box in his hands. I released John's hands.

"So what now?" Ty asked, arching his eyebrows.

John was silent, and I thought for a moment.

"This needs to go back home," I said, taking the box from Ty. It felt warm from his touch. "It should go back to France. I'll contact the French consulate in San Francisco and have them determine where such an important historical piece should go."

"And then?" Ty asked.

"We take it there ourselves. And you, too, John, if you want. You're a big part of this story, and I'd like you to be there for its final chapter."

Hoffmann smiled and nodded.

"Again, I'd be honored," he said, gesturing for us to follow him back to his office. "Let me know what the consulate tells you, and we'll coordinate. After all this, I suspect we could all use a nice trip to France."

CHAPTER 20

Two weeks later, Ty and I were at SFO boarding a flight for Orly. The box was in his carry-on backpack, along with an official document from the French Embassy for the TSA, stating that we were transporting an important historical item for delivery to a museum in Paris.

This allowed us to keep it with us for safekeeping, although we got an attitude from the TSA agent who processed us. He huffed when he looked at Ty's passport, which still had his photo from Eros, with long hair and no beard. The agent looked up at him, squinting.

"So this is supposed to be you?" he sniped, catching the attention of the female agent next to him.

She moved over and looked at the photo, giving a slight gasp and smiling broadly as she looked up at Ty

."It's okay, Mitchell," she said, taking the passport and handing it back to Ty. "It's him."

She looked at Ty intently. Obviously a fan. She reached out and they shook hands, then she asked for a selfie with the new Tyler Powell. That made him smile.

The flight was long and uneventful. Ty spent a lot of it on his laptop, in an app he used to write music. Since the Flamel mystery had been winding down, he'd been spending a great deal of time in the studio, composing and recording, and would soon have his new work ready for release.

He was understandably nervous about that, about whether his Eros fans would accept him as he now was, but we'd already been able to see on social media how the buzz was starting to build. His fans were actually eager to see and hear the new Tyler, and I reminded him of that whenever he waffled about acceptance.

I'd be interested to hear what this new "sky song" was when we got home.

It was late afternoon by the time we got to our Paris hotel. We went up to our room, and called John on his cell phone. He and his wife Catherine were in a room several doors down the hall from us, and we decided we'd meet in an hour to go out to dinner together.

We met up with them in the hotel lobby, and John came over to me, giving me a hug and shaking Tyler's hand. His wife, a beautiful lady with silver-white hair, gave both of us the standard two-cheek kiss. As we were introduced, we found out that she was actually French by birth, and would be very useful in acting as interpreter as needed.

"Where shall we go?" John asked.

"Well, I did a little research," I answered, smiling. "Nearby, at 51 rue de Montmorency, is the house Flamel and his wife built and lived in. The ground floor has been a restaurant for many years, so I thought it would be fitting for us to eat there, then check out the rest of the building. I corresponded with the restaurant owner, who's given his permission for us to do that."

"How cool!" Ty exclaimed.

He had a leather shoulder bag that carried the box. In my planning for this dinner, I had decided it would be fitting to return Nicolas and Perenelle's letters to their home, albeit just for a few minutes. An emotional and romantic thing for me to come up with, but I figured it was a result of the way my relationship with Tyler was softening me, smoothing the rough edges of the personality I'd created for myself early on.

I didn't need to be the tough, hard-as-nails bitch I'd always felt I had to be. It was a good feeling to let go of many of those expectations I'd had of myself for so long to be totally independent, needing no one else.

I'd now come to realize that I needed Ty as much as he needed me.

It was getting dark when we arrived at the building by taxi. It was a fairly unremarkable building at first glance, but the plaque on the front, headed "Maison de Nicolas Flamel", indicated in French (and interpreted by Catherine) that the house was actually the oldest stone building still standing in the city of Paris, built in 1407. Impressive, Nicolas!

We entered and were greeted by the restaurant owner I'd been corresponding with. We agreed to eat first and then he would show us the rest of the house afterward.

The dining area was an amazing example of the architecture of Flamel's time, with heavy, dark beams contrasted by white walls. It reminded me a bit of our Tudor, strangely enough.

Dinner was excellent French food accented by enjoyable conversation among the four of us. Catherine expressed her thanks that we'd helped her husband move past the issue his father had burdened his life with. She'd known about it and his true identity for many years, and had always hoped something would eventually happen to relieve him of that heavy psychological burden.

When we finished our meal, our host showed us up the nearby staircase to Flamel's living quarters. Things had not changed very much, although some updating had been done. As we approached what the owner told us had been the Flamels' bedroom, I had an odd feeling wash over me. I stopped Ty and asked him to pull the box out of his shoulder bag. He handed it to me.

The owner opened the door to reveal a simply furnished bedroom, with a bed, wardrobe, vanity, and a desk with an oil lamp. For a moment I visualized Flamel seated at that desk, quill in hand, writing one of the letters in the box I held. It was a surreal feeling.

I set the box down on the desk.

"You've come full circle," I said quietly, my left hand resting on the top of the box.

I stood there for a couple of minutes. We were all quiet, savoring this moment when history was, in a sense, cycling back around. I picked up the box, tucked it back into the shoulder bag, and we all went back downstairs.

"Catherine and I are going to go back to the hotel," John said as we headed to the door. "We're not as young as you two, so we're going to get some rest for tomorrow. Good night, my friends."

We all hugged our goodbyes and walked out to the street. The Hoffmanns got into a taxi and Ty and I stood, looking at each other.

"It's still early, and we're on California time, so do you want to check out a club or something?" he asked, shifting the bag on his shoulder. "There's a blues club I went to once that's near the hotel. It's pretty cool."

"Sure, but let's stop by the hotel and have them put the box back in their safe. I don't want to be carting it around."

So we spent the rest of the evening at the blues club, drinking beer and enjoying the well-known enthusiasm of European club-goers for American blues. We'd been there for about an hour when, despite his shorter hair and beard, Ty was recognized by a couple of people, and word spread as to who he was.

I had to smile when the band on stage asked him in broken English to please come up and do one of his Eros songs. Apparently they were fans of Eros and included a bluesy cover of one of his songs in their set. They were thrilled to have Ty willing to get up there and sing his lead. The one song turned into a mini jam session, Ty picking up the guitar player's secondary axe and going for it with the gusto of a man who's seriously missed live performance.

Everyone was having a ball, and phones were busy all through the venue, recording the surprise visit of Tyler Powell to this Paris blues club. And I was doing it, too. I wanted him to be able to watch it himself later at the hotel.

It was great fun, very satisfying for Ty, and, once word got out, it would be great publicity. Then an idea struck me. I waved at him and caught his attention on the stage.

I cupped my mouth with my hands and mouthed "New song!" to him.

He smiled broadly back at me and gave a thumbs up. then stepped over to the band and we all watched as they huddled for a minute. Obviously, he was asking them if it was okay if he played one of his new songs. Their body language told me they were more than happy.

The band's lead went up to the microphone and told the crowd they were about to be the first to hear Tyler Powell's new song that would soon be released as a single. The crowd went crazy. I think I must have smiled in that moment as much as Ty did.

He switched out the electric guitar for an acoustic and stepped up to the mic. Knowing him as I now did, I could feel the nervousness in him. Again worrying about acceptance.

The spotlight focused on him and he began. It was one of his more upbeat pieces, and he'd chosen it to be his first release. Everyone was watching and listening quietly, relishing that they were the first.

He finished the song, lowered his right hand from the strings, and stood there. It was silent. For about ten seconds. Then the crowd went, as Nick would have said, "banana-fish". They'd loved it, big time.

Ty's face was beaming. He put down the guitar and came down toward me, giving high-fives and handshakes as he came through the audience. When he got to me, I gave him an "I told you so" look with a smile, and he pulled me into his arms.

"I should never, ever doubt you, love," he said, giving me a kiss, which got a whoop from the crowd.

We stayed for about another hour, talking with people, taking selfies, and just enjoying the whole moment.

I could feel Ty's happiness. This spontaneous night had told us that everything was going to be good. Better than good.

CHAPTER 21

The next morning, as we had a light breakfast in our room, Ty went on his laptop to check emails and his social media.

His fan page had blown up with comments on the videos the French fans had posted overnight. The YouTube posts had already been moving up toward a quarter of a million views total. It was crazy.

"I knew you needn't have worried," I said, standing behind him with my arms around his shoulders and crossing in front of him. "They love you, not just Eros. It was always *you*."

He reached up and took one of my hands, kissing it. He looked back at me.

"Thank you for being my rock. You've had faith in me when I didn't. And you were right."

That was one of the most gratifying moments I'd ever had in my life.

We met up with the Hoffmann's in the hotel lobby and got into a taxi that would take us to the Musee Carnavalet not far away. That was where the consulate had determined, after negotiating with the cultural and historical organizations in Paris, the box would be taken, studied and documented before being delivered to its final museum home. We'd looked it up online, and it was a beautiful group of buildings, iconically French, with extraordinary gardens and sculptured grounds. We hoped to be able to take some time to stroll around it after dropping off Flamel's box.

However...

"Oh no!" I exclaimed as our taxi approached the entrance to the m useum.There were at least twenty media people crowded there, cameras at the ready. My three companions looked at me.

"I told the consulate no media coverage!" I said, clapping my left hand to my forehead in frustration. "We just wanted a quiet transition, but somebody obviously leaked it. Damn! I'm sorry, all of you. This isn't how I wanted it to happen."

"It's all right," John said, patting my hand. "Don't worry yourself about it."

"John's right," Ty said, taking my hand in his. "Time to make some lemonade."

We seemed to have been doing that a lot, making lemonade out of the lemons we had so often found ourselves buried in, but so far it had always worked out. I hoped this would be another of those times.

I couldn't tell during the minutes that followed if the media was there for the cultural significance of the Flamel box, or for Tyler Powell's involvement. While one of the museum officials was there to greet us and answer the media's questions, most of the questions were being levied at Tyler about our visit to the blues club the night before.While that was going to be great publicity for him, I found myself feeling annoyed that our reason for being there was not the main focus. So I stepped over to the museum official and whispered in her ear that I wanted to move it inside where we could have privacy for the giving over of the Flamel artifact.

She smiled and nodded, and we walked toward the museum entrance, the box cradled in my arms. John and Catherine followed. Ty was stuck in the middle of a gaggle. He'd get loose soon enough. As we headed into an ornate, terribly cliché French parlor, Ty caught up with us, after breaking free of the reporters. He didn't want to miss the moment, nor had we wanted anything to happen until he was there. The museum had one staff videographer there to capture the event - the low-key approach I'd wanted.

It was a brief, simple ceremony, the museum official thanking us on behalf of the French people for returning the Flamel box and letters to his country after such a long absence. We gave our permission for them to post the video and photographs on the museum website.

An episode closed.

A decades-long mystery that had been twisted into knots was now untangled and finally resolved.

When we finished the ceremony, we were ushered to a back entrance, where two taxis awaited. John and Catherine got into one after we said our goodbyes, and Ty and I into the other.

"Take us somewhere along the Seine where we can walk," he told the driver.

Several minutes later, we got out of the taxi and walked over to a beautiful riverside promenade. The sun was bright on the water, and the air smelled of flowers and aromas from nearby restaurants. We stopped and looked across the river at the centuries-old buildings that Paris was so appropriately known for. Ty put his arm around my shoulder, glanced at me, then looked back out across the river.

"I had a talk with Nick before we left to come to Paris," he said quietly. "I wanted to get his input on something and apparently it was good that I did. Otherwise, I could have made a huge mistake I'd never want to make."

I looked up at him.

"Is there something wrong?"

"No, not wrong," he answered, looking in my eyes. "Just, I don't know, perplexing."

"You need to give me more than that. Just tell me."

"Okay. We were coming to romantic Paris. I've been here on a few tours, but I only ever saw the hotels, restaurants and venues, never the city itself. Coming here with you, I was finally going to be able to do that. I wanted to make it even more special than that. I was going to ask you to marry me."

Shocked, I forced myself to keep my cool.

"And Nick warned you, didn't he?"

"Yeah. He told me you wouldn't because you personally believe marriage is outdated and unnecessary, right?"

"That's pretty much it, yes. At least it is for me."

"I guess I'm just a helpless, hapless romantic," he said, turning me to face him. He touched my cheek. "It wasn't until I met you that I could see what I'd been missing in my life. Yeah, there was a lot of sex, but that's all it was. There was no real affection, no honest love. I couldn't see that I was empty, until you came along.

"So what I *am* going to do is tell you how completely I need you. We're together. That's what I want. That's all I need."

Tears appeared in the corners of his eyes. I was speechless. No man had ever hit me point-blank like that, and I didn't know how to respond.

Why was I so afraid of agreeing with him? He was letting me have my way about marriage, so why not accept that he just wanted us to be together? Surely that's what I wanted, too. I wouldn't give up a moment of the time we'd had in the last few months. It was precious, and he was precious. More than precious.

So what was wrong with me that I couldn't just come out and tell this man that I loved and needed him the same way he said he loved and needed me?

I wanted to say it, but I just couldn't, and I didn't know why.

It didn't make sense. I made love with him, I cooked with him, ate meals with him, shared his house, shared his bed, shared our lives. And my university psycho-babble was just confusing me more.

This was a man who could have any woman he wanted, for god's sake, and I was still amazed that who he wanted was crazy, headstrong, stubborn *me*. It just didn't seem real. Maybe that was part of the problem - fear that this reality would fall away at some point, and me with it.

So instead of opening my heart as I should have, I simply smiled and kissed him.

On the romantic banks of the Seine, I couldn't bring myself to tell the man I loved that I did.

I felt like a damned coward and couldn't understand why I was such a big one.

END

If you loved **"The Box,"** then you will want to read **"The Road."** Book 3 in the The Phaedra Chronicle series.

Phaedra feeling adrift.

Tyler reclaiming and reinventing himself.

A new adventure, together.

A threat she must deal with head-on.

Reconciliation?

"The Phaedra Chronicles - The Road" follows the evolving relationship between Phaedra and Tyler, as they each search for what their futures can be, both together and individually.

While Phaedra steps away from the career she'd always planned, she soon finds a situation arise in which she has to use her experience in that career to protect her lover. She won't let anyone hurt him in any way.

And when she's talked into visiting her dying mother, can she set aside her feelings of hatred for a mother who had always so completely disregarded and insulted her, and attempt a reconciliation?

Made in the USA
Las Vegas, NV
29 January 2024

85021752R00083